ALWAYS HAVE

ALWAYS SERIES BOOK 1

CLAIRE KINGSLEY

Always Have LLC

Copyright © 2016 Claire Kingsley

All rights reserved.

No part of this book may be reproduced in any form or by any electronic or mechanical means, including information storage and retrieval systems, without written permission from the author, except for the use of brief quotations in a book review.

This is a work of fiction. Any names, characters, places, or incidents are products of the author's imagination and used in a fictitious manner. Any resemblance to actual people, places, or events is purely coincidental or fictionalized.

Published by Always Have, LLC

Edited by Larks and Katydids

Cover by Lori Jackson

ISBN: 9798332278655

www.clairekingsleybooks.com

❦ Created with Vellum

ABOUT THIS BOOK

Kylie's best friend Braxton is the hottest man she's ever known, with a rock hard body and a smile that melts the panties off every woman he meets.

Except Kylie. Mostly.

Kylie is anxious to get off the dating carousel and find something real. Despite the way Braxton tends to suck the air from her lungs, she knows he's trouble. He's just another player, and she's tired of the game.

But Braxton isn't the man she thinks.

The real reason he's sh*t with women is simple. None of the women he's with are the one he wants. None of them are Kylie.

He wants to love her in every way imaginable, but there's always something in the way. So he stays her friend, watching her date men who are too stupid to realize how special she is. Always worried the next one won't be. The next one will be the man who takes her from him forever.

Loving Kylie risks every fiber of their friendship, but losing her might be more than Braxton can take.

1

KYLIE

Ten minutes to midnight, and I have no idea where my date is.

That's the problem with letting your best friend set you up with someone for a New Year's Eve party. It's such a date sort of holiday, with all the pressure to have someone to kiss at midnight. I'm surrounded by couples—drinking, talking, kissing, slipping hands in naughty places when they think no one is looking—but I'm leaning against the kitchen island at my best friend Selene's house, looking like an idiot as I comb the party for … what was his name?

Steven. Right, it's Steven.

Things started off well enough. He showed up looking nice in a blue sweater and jeans. Clean-cut, smooth jaw. All in all, not a bad looking guy. I'm rocking a black mini-dress and a pair of fantastic red heels—because why not, it's a holiday, and my red heels are hot. I wore my dark hair down and wavy, which makes me feel sexy, and I think I've finally perfected that smoky eye thing without making myself look like I got punched in the face. The way Steven's gaze moved up and down when Selene introduced us, he seemed to like what he saw. We grabbed a couple drinks and made semi-awkward conversation, the way you do when you're both the victims of a set-up and aren't quite sure if agreeing was a good idea.

Two drinks in, he was leaning closer, and he did smell good. He said he's an accountant, and I had to stop myself from choking on my beer. Selene set me up with an accountant? Then again, I was just telling her that I need to stop dating the wrong guys. Hot men with killer abs who are stallions in bed are *fun*, but they're not necessarily the kind you bring home to meet your father. And as much as I do not want to admit it, I'm not in my early twenties anymore. Hell, I've passed my mid-twenties at this point, and thirty is getting awfully close. I feel like maybe it's time to get serious about this adulting thing—quit chasing the bad boys with fabulous cocks, and find someone responsible. Mature. In fact, it's one of my new year's resolutions.

Steven seemed like he fit the bill, although the more we chatted the more I realized I felt absolutely nothing for him. No desire to inch closer and accidentally-on-purpose brush against him. No temptation to tilt my chin up and lick my lips to draw attention to my mouth. No finding excuses to put my hand on his arm.

I was kind of bored.

Still, that's no excuse for the guy to wander off and ditch me just before midnight.

Music blares through the speakers; the living room turned into a dance floor about an hour ago. I see Selene, swaying to the music with her boyfriend Nathan. It's a fast song with a good beat, but they're acting like two kids at prom, slow dancing as if no one else is around. I'm happy for Selene. I wasn't so sure about Nathan at first. He struck me as too much the bad boy type—or, more accurately, the

Selene type, which is not necessarily a good thing—but he actually seems pretty nice.

Selene's been my best friend since we were kids; my father was their family's lawyer. She and her twin brother Braxton lost their parents when they were ten, and my dad saw to the estate and managed the trust that contained their parents' considerable fortune. It meant I spent a lot of time roaming around their big house, the three of us getting into all sorts of trouble together. Over the years, we've stayed close. If anything, we're better friends as adults than we were as scabby-kneed kids.

I search the crowd for Steven again and see Hope trying to murder me with her eyes. Hope is Braxton's girlfriend, and she hates me with a seething passion I can feel from across the room. I pretend I don't notice her. She's disliked me from the first time we met, about a month ago. I don't let her ire concern me in the least. This is Braxton we're talking about. Braxton's relationships never last. He's way too much of a player to stick with anyone.

I give Hope another month, two if she sucks his dick regularly.

Still, I don't understand why she hates *me* so much, other than the fact that I'm Braxton's best friend. She must assume that means friends with benefits. It's never been that way with me and Brax, though. We've never even fooled around. It's one of the main tenets of our friendship—the thing that makes this guy/girl thing work, despite the fact that Braxton seems to want to stick his dick in half the women in Seattle. He and I don't cross that line.

Not that I haven't considered it. Braxton isn't the type of man you can be around without thinking about what it would be like to kiss him. Or fuck him. Because if there's any man in this world who is totally and completely fuckable, it's Braxton Taylor.

But I leave that to the steady stream of women who flit in and out of his life, and keep him firmly in the friend zone.

Selene and Nathan wander over from the makeshift dance floor. Selene's house is amazing. She still lives in the house she and Braxton grew up in, a fucking mansion in Phinney Ridge. Braxton insisted she keep it, and after college he bought himself a condo not far from here, just off Greenwood. The house is deceiving from the outside. It's like one of those magical Harry Potter tents—looks pretty normal from the street, but once you walk in, it's breathtaking. It has six bedrooms, a huge living, dining, and kitchen area with soaring ceilings, an old-fashioned study, and great views from upstairs. Braxton and I don't live here, but we still have our own bedrooms, leftover from our college days. Selene used to bug me about moving back in with her—the house is definitely way too big for one person—but I prefer to live on my own. There's a certain weirdness in leaning on their money, even though both of them have plenty. I have an apartment about ten minutes away, but I crash here when the occasion arises. I definitely will tonight—although, sadly, it appears I'll be sleeping alone.

Selene stands next to me while Nathan pours drinks at the counter.

"Awesome night, huh?" she says. "Where's Steven?"

She looks glorious in a shimmering, sleeveless gold top and black skirt, with her brown hair pinned up. She has a Victoria's Secret model body—tall and effortlessly thin, with fantastic boobs.

"I don't know," I say. "I guess he went to the bathroom or something."

"Well, you better find him," Selene says. "It's almost midnight."

Someone turns on the flat screen to the New Year's countdown. Nathan hands Selene her drink and they go back into the midst of the party.

I decide to do a lap to see if I can find this date of mine. The least the guy can do is make sure I'm not the only one at this party standing alone to ring in the new year. We don't have to make out, but someone to clink glasses with would be nice. He didn't even tell me where he was going; he just mumbled something about being right back. That was at least ten minutes ago.

I don't see him among the people dancing, and he isn't grazing on the snacks set out in the dining room. The downstairs bathroom is empty, although a girl ducks in front of me and darts in, closing the door behind her. The study door is closed—Selene doesn't usually want guests in there—but I peek inside, just in case. It's empty. I check my bedroom, which isn't far from the kitchen. No one in there either.

I walk to the entry foyer and find a couple making out next to the coat rack, but neither of them are Steven. I don't know why he'd go upstairs, but I figure I'll check. The wide staircase curves to an upper balcony. I take another look from the top, but don't see him anywhere.

The music is quieter upstairs, and I hear the distinct sound of moaning. Oh lord, am I about to walk in on someone getting it on in the hallway? Are we at a fucking frat party? It's dark, but I walk a little farther and definitely see someone—two someones. The guy has the girl pressed up against the wall, his hand up her shirt. She's giggling as he kisses down her neck.

I don't want to intrude, so I'm just about to hightail it

back downstairs when I recognize the guy's sweater. Wasn't Steven wearing blue? There's not much light but—

He turns his head just enough, and I get a glimpse of his face. It's definitely Steven.

I back up quickly, tip-toeing so they won't notice me. Fuck. Of course my date would make out with some other woman at the New Year's party. That pretty much sums up my love life right there.

So much for the responsible and mature accountant.

I head back downstairs, planning to retreat to my room. Selene will ask about Steven if she sees me, and I don't want to ruin her night by telling her what happened. I'll make her feel guilty about setting me up with a douchebag later. Tonight is her party, and I don't want to mess it up for her.

I slip through the kitchen to get another beer, then pause and think better of it. Instead, I grab a plastic cup and mix an impromptu cocktail. Vodka, over ice—and I may or may not tip in a little extra after I pour in two shots. I add some cranberry juice from the fridge. There. That ought to keep me company while I listen to the happy people out here, starting their new year off right.

"Hey, Ky," a gravelly voice says behind me. "Where you running off to?"

"Hey, Braxton," I say.

Selene's twin brother looks so much like her. They have the same dark eyes, olive skin, dark hair. But where Selene is tall and slender—she's a fucking Amazon warrior at five-eleven—Braxton is six-foot-four-inches of thick, solid muscle.

He quirks an eyebrow at me. "Where's your, uh ... date?"

"Found someone else to hang out with."

Braxton's expression darkens. "Seriously?"

"Yeah," I say with a shrug. Despite the fact that I wasn't

into Steven, being ditched still stings. But I don't want Braxton to know that. "Whatever. He was boring anyway."

Braxton moves a little closer and I catch a whiff of him. I swear, the guy must have a cologne called *Weak Knees*. I always feel fluttery in the stomach when he's around, always need a minute or two to find my grounding. It must be why he gets so much ass.

"He left you alone right before midnight?"

"Yeah, it's no big deal."

I glance around, looking for Hope, but she's nowhere in sight. I want to ask Braxton how much longer I'll have to deal with her murder glares, but I don't. It would violate our unspoken pact, the other tenet that makes our friendship work: we don't talk about our relationships, especially if we don't like whoever the other person is dating—which is pretty much always. When a relationship ends, the pact is nullified, and the gloves come off. But prior to that, our dates are off limits.

This came about because the people we date are never comfortable with our friendship. Hope isn't unique in that. No one minds Selene—Braxton's girlfriends want to impress her and become her BFF. My dates see how hot she is, and try to hide it when they stare, but they don't mind me spending time with her. But Brax always seems like a threat, and apparently so do I.

Why his girlfriends see me that way, I have no idea. The women he's with are always more like Selene than me—tall, model gorgeous, with great clothes and perfect hair. I'm just ... me. I'm happy with how I look, but I'm not going to grace the covers of magazines or anything. I'm average height, and a little too curvy for my taste these days (did I mention I am no longer in my early twenties?). I do have a nice rack, but I'm not crazy gorgeous or anything.

But Braxton? I get it. I don't blame any guy I date for being uncomfortable with our friendship. Braxton is big and powerful, and not just physically. He's one of those people who fills whatever space he's in. His personality is as big as his biceps—maybe bigger.

And he's fucking gorgeous. I can admit that to myself, although I'd *never* tell him. He has a strong jaw that he keeps covered in light stubble. His eyes are so dark they're almost black, and when he stares at you, it's like he can see through to your soul. He's just the right type of muscular—big and strong, without looking like a meathead. He has a set of gorgeous tattoos down his left arm, adding to the bad boy thing he does so well. Women stare at him wherever he goes, and he knows it. Women are putty for him.

Except me, of course.

Mostly.

"That sucks," he says. "You shouldn't start the new year without someone to properly kiss that sweet mouth."

Hope is definitely not around, and Braxton is definitely drunk.

I smile and take a sip of my drink so he'll quit looking at my mouth. I hate it when he looks at me like this; I feel like I can't breathe. "That's okay," I say. "I'll be fine. It's a stupid holiday anyway. Who fucking cares? It's just a calendar flip. It's not like a new year has to mean anything."

I'm lying through my teeth. I've been looking forward to this night for the last month, feeling like this coming year will be different. I'm going to get my shit together and start living life on my terms. Set goals. Find a better job. Achieve things I can be proud of. Maybe find love—real love, with a future. Not this dating bullshit, with the games and uncertainty.

I've been planning to make this a year of change, a year

of figuring out my shit. Which is probably why the fact that I'm about to sneak off to my room and start the new year by myself, nursing a strong drink, brings the sting of tears to my eyes.

Someone yells, "One minute!"

Braxton gets closer. "You need someone to kiss tonight, Ky?"

I force out a laugh. "Why, you offering?"

He meets my eyes and, for a second, I think he's serious. My smile drops and my heart beats too fast.

"There you are," Hope says, slipping her hand around Braxton's arm. "It's almost time."

He steps back, his expression mischievous. He was totally fucking with me. I let out the breath I didn't realize I was holding.

"Come on, baby," Hope says, trying to pull him out of the kitchen. Her eyes narrow at me, but her expression softens before Braxton sees the look she gives me.

Everyone starts counting down. "Ten ... nine ... eight..."

I watch Braxton for a beat longer as he lets Hope lead him away. He turns to her and puts his hand around her waist while she tips her face up to him, ready for his kiss. People around them pair off. Selene and Nathan are already busy playing tongue hockey on the other side of the room.

"Six ... five ... four..."

I can't even deal with this scene. Clutching my cup, I cross the distance to my room and duck inside. I lean back against the door just in time to hear, "One!"

Cheers. Noisemakers. Whoops and hollers. I'm sure Braxton is kissing Hope, a prelude to him tossing her over his shoulder and carrying her upstairs to his room. I'll probably have to suffer her dirty looks through breakfast tomorrow. Maybe I'll get up early and go home before Braxton and

Selene wake up. I'm not sure I want to hang out with people who all got laid the night before, while I'm spending the night alone in my room, with only my good friend vodka to keep me company.

I sink down on the bed and put the drink on the nightstand. As much as I want this year to be better, from the way it's beginning I'm pretty sure it's going to be a lot more of the same.

2

BRAXTON

My phone vibrates in my hand and I smile, seeing the text is from Kylie.

I assume you have plans, but if not—date-free Valentine's Day dinner. Just us three. Wanna come?

Sounds fucking perfect to me. I broke up with Hope a few days ago. She didn't exactly take it well. I guess I'm a dick for breaking up with her right before Valentine's Day. There was quite a bit of yelling, a slap that stung my cheek, and a lot of broken glass for me to clean up when she finally left.

Hope was definitely a firecracker. It was one of the things I liked about her, but there was a downside to her spirit. Hope will be fine. She's hot as hell, and she could do a lot better than an asshole like me anyway.

I answer Kylie's text, realizing it's been a while since I could text back and forth with her without angling my phone so my jealous girlfriend can't see who I'm talking to.

You know I'm in, baby girl.

It's going to be a relief to be able to shamelessly flirt with Kylie again. She's one of the reasons I broke it off with Hope, although I would never admit that to either of them. I knew Hope didn't like Kylie. She seemed to think I didn't see her glaring, but I'm not blind. It pissed me off. If a girl can't handle my friendship with Kylie, they need to step off. I put up with Hope's jealousy for a while—she gave me some very compelling reasons, and I don't mean with words—but it got old.

Not that I blame her. It's not easy to be with a guy who has a close relationship with another woman. Particularly when that woman is Kylie. She's fucking adorable. She's one of those women who has absolutely no clue how beautiful she is, and that only makes her hotter. She's little compared to me and Selene, with inky dark hair, and these crazy blue-gray eyes, plus a tight round ass and a set of magnificent tits.

Yes, I notice her ass and her tits. Of course I do. I'm a fucking man, aren't I?

I'm normally not the kind of guy who gives a crap about Valentine's Day, but since I get to hang out with my sister and Kylie, sans boyfriends or dates, I'm in a pretty good mood about it. I wonder why Selene isn't going out with that Nathan guy, but I guess I'll find out tonight. I'm assuming it isn't because they broke up, otherwise I would have heard. I decide to swing by a store and get them both flowers. That will make them smile.

I meet my girls at a Thai place not far from my condo. I saunter back to their table, holding two huge bouquets of roses wrapped in white paper—pink for Selene, red for Ky. Selene sees me first and her face lights up.

I grin at both of them. "Ladies," I say, and hand them their flowers.

"Aw," Selene says. She takes the flowers and holds them up to smell them. "Big brother, you're the sweetest."

We're twins, but I'm older by three minutes.

"And for you," I say, handing the red bouquet to Kylie.

Kylie takes the flowers, but looks more suspicious than my sister. "What is this all about?"

"It's Valentine's Day," I say. "I wanted to make sure my girls had flowers."

They're sitting on the same side of the table, so I take a seat across from them.

"So how are we all dateless tonight?" Kylie asks.

"Nathan is out of town for work," Selene says. "I was kind of bummed about it, but this is fun."

Kylie's eyes flit to me. She won't ask. She'll wait to see if I mention why I'm not taking Hope out tonight. It's our thing. We don't discuss our relationships.

"Hope and I broke up," I say with a shrug.

"That's too bad," Selene says.

Kylie raises an eyebrow. "Is it?"

"Oh, come on, Ky," Selene says, "Hope wasn't so bad."

"She hated my guts," Kylie says.

My stomach twists a little at that. Kylie did notice. Fuck, that pisses me off. "Yeah, well, it's over. So we can celebrate our singlehood together tonight."

"You guys go ahead," Selene says with a smug smile. "I'm very happily un-single at the moment."

"I like Nathan," Kylie says. "At first I thought he was too arrogant, but he's actually pretty funny. I'm glad things are working out for you guys."

Selene smiles, and my heart swells. I love seeing my sister happy. Nathan better not fuck this up, though, or I'll break his face.

The waitress arrives with our dinners, setting down a steaming plate of food in front of each of us.

"Crispy garlic chicken with sautéed basil, five star," Kylie says, pointing to my dinner. "I ordered for you."

"Thanks, Ky," I say. The smell already burns my nose. I love Thai food, and crispy garlic chicken is one of my favorites at this place. Kylie knows me well.

We all dig into our dinners. Selene has some sort of veggie thing that looks decent, but Kylie ordered coconut curry chicken, which is my second favorite thing here. I reach over and grab a bite from her plate. It has just the right mix of heat and flavor.

"The cook is serious with the spice tonight," I say.

Kylie samples from my plate and makes an approving yummy noise.

"So what's going on with that guy you were trying to sign?" Selene asks.

"Derek Marshall? Oh, he'll sign," I say. I'm an athletic trainer, specializing in college and pro athletes. My soon-to-be client is a receiver for the Seahawks. He's trying to up his game after he almost got traded last season, which is where I come in. "He knows I'm the best. His manager is being a pain the ass about it, but he'll come around."

"Why does his manager care who trains him in the offseason?" Selene asks.

"Who the fuck knows," I say. "Maybe he's getting kickbacks from the current trainer and he knows I don't play like that."

Getting a Seahawk as a client, especially one as high-profile as Derek Marshall, will be great for my business. I have a lot of clients in other pro sports—soccer and baseball in particular. But football is my personal favorite, so I'd love to train more players. A football career was once my dream for my future, but a motorcycle accident when I was eighteen put an end to that.

Kylie's phone goes off and she digs it out of her purse to

check. A little smile crosses her face as she reads her message.

"What's up?" Selene asks.

"You remember that guy I went out with a week or so ago?" she asks.

"The one who was so much fun, and then you didn't hear from him after your first date?" Selene asks. She sounds as skeptical as I feel. If the guy's ignoring Kylie, she should fucking ignore him right back.

"Yeah, but he says he didn't call because he had to go out of town for a family emergency," Kylie says. She smiles again. "He apologized for not calling and says he wants to see me this weekend."

I keep my face carefully neutral. I think it's bullshit, but I don't say anything. Family emergency, my ass.

"Are you going to?" Selene asks.

"Yeah," Kylie says, as she types. "We had fun. And he was definitely fuckable. I'll see where this goes."

Hearing her say *fuckable* makes my back clench and I almost drop my fork. I hate this guy already. I don't know who he is, but I'd like to smash his face in right now.

She puts her phone away, still smiling. "Awesome. Now I'm excited for Friday."

"Hey, if you guys hit it off, we should triple date," Selene says. "Maybe in a couple weeks?"

"Triple date?" I ask, raising an eyebrow. "Who the fuck is the triple? Because, hey, single again."

"Whatever, Brax," Selene says. "Like you won't be screwing some girl by then."

I shrug my shoulders. I guess she's probably right.

We finish our dinners, Kylie and I taking bites from each other's plates. I ask if they want to go out for a drink, but they both have to work in the morning, so we part ways outside. Kylie drove, so I watch until I see her get in her car.

Selene gets a call from Nathan and she waves at me absently as she walks away. I'd walk her home, but she only lives a few blocks away, and it annoys her when I try to do stuff like that. She says I'm overprotective, but that's total bullshit. She's my sister. There's no such thing as overprotective when it comes to her.

I'm restless and I don't feel like going home, so I round the corner and pop into a bar. Kevin, the bartender, knows me, and he tips his head when I walk in.

My gaze immediately lands on the group of women sitting at a table on the far side. I'll bet a thousand dollars it's an anti-Valentine's Day outing. Group of single girls, showing their *we don't need men* solidarity by going out drinking on this bullshit holiday.

They might think they don't need men, but one of them is coming home with me.

I sit down at the bar and order a beer, but angle myself so I can watch them. I don't bother to hide that I'm checking them out. Three of the four are hot enough to take home, but one in particular catches my eye. Long legs, straight hair, full lips. She's exactly the type of girl I usually go after: tall, blond, nice boobs. It's an easy sell for me. You might think that's my type, but the truth is, it isn't. But it is the type I go for to get my mind off my real type.

Because my real type—the woman I want more than anything—I can't have. She's my best friend. And she's always been off limits.

I fell for Kylie, hard, when we were teenagers. Fuck, it was before that, but at ten or eleven years old I hardly knew what the feeling was. I knew I loved it when she came over. I found out where my Aunt Cindy kept her day planner, and

I'd sneak it to look for the appointments with Mr. Winters, our family lawyer. If Mr. Winters was coming over, that meant he'd bring Kylie. He always did.

I'd wait for her at the top of the staircase like a fucking puppy. She'd walk in the door and the world would get a little brighter. The pain of losing my parents wasn't quite so bad when she was around. It was the only time I was really happy.

By the time we were teenagers, the three of us still hung out all the time, although we went to different schools. I watched her developing body with keen interest and a fair amount of confusion as to what was happening to mine when I thought of her. And that's when it started—the shitty timing. She came over one day and pulled Selene aside, the two of them talking in excited whispers.

Kylie had a boyfriend. He'd kissed her on the mouth. With tongues. I pretended I didn't care, that it didn't cut through me like a fucking butcher knife. I made a joke about the size of her new boyfriend's dick, and she was mad at me for weeks. So I never commented on her boyfriends again.

Relationships came and went, for both of us. I started dating girls; they weren't her, so nothing lasted. I got a reputation as a player, and I went with it. Might as well. It's all part of the facade, the mask I wear to be the man the two women in my life need me to be. Selene needs me to be her strong guy, her rock, her protector. So I am. Kylie needs me to be her friend. So that's what I am for her. And if that's all I ever get to be, then I'll take it and consider myself fucking lucky. Because being her friend is a hell of a lot better than not having her in my life at all.

That's what I tell myself, at least.

But as time goes on, it's getting harder to keep it inside. I love every second I get to spend with her, but at the same time, it's torture. I've watched her date assholes who don't appreciate her, and some who almost do—and those are the ones who scare the fuck out of me. We're both nearing thirty, and one of these days, she's going to meet the guy who will capture her heart and take her from me forever.

I have no idea what to do about that.

I don't interfere with her relationships. Just a text asking for a date, like the one she got at dinner tonight, is enough to send me retreating back behind my protective wall. I live behind that wall, never letting the world see the man I am inside. It's tall and thick as fuck, built of hard stone and painful loss. I'm the man my girls need me to be. Nothing more.

So instead, I look for happiness, or some version of it, and usually just find a lot of empty sex that makes me feel like shit when it's over. I don't talk to my girls about that either. They see what I want them to see—the big, confident asshole who can turn any woman into water in the blink of an eye. And I am that guy. He isn't an act or a lie. But he's not *all* of me.

Tonight, because the ache in my chest is too much to bear, I let him take the lead.

I take a long pull from the bottle and turn my attention back to the blonde at the table. I catch her eye and offer a very small smile. Just a twitch of my lips. She looks down quickly, like she's going to play shy.

Most guys would order her a drink and have it sent over. I don't play that game. I'll make eye contact a few times, show her I'm interested. If she approaches me, great—I like it when women are bold. If not, I'll just walk up and tell her what I want.

I don't get turned down very often.

I glance at their table again. They're all looking at me now. I focus on the blonde, holding her gaze for a long moment. The others giggle a little and whisper behind their hands.

I take a swig of my beer. Might as well get this show on the road.

"Evening, ladies," I say as I approach the table. I hold my hand out to the blonde. She takes it and I lean in, bringing her fingers up to my lips. "Braxton Taylor. And you are?"

She looks at me with an open mouth. Yep, she's in. I can see the *yes* in her eyes.

"Jessica," she says.

I keep hold of her hand. "It is very nice to meet you, Jessica."

Her friends are staring at me, just as open-mouthed as she is.

"You, too," Jessica says, her voice breathy.

I hesitate for half a second, wondering if I should ask her over to the bar to get her away from the influence of her friends, or just say fuck it and proposition her right here. I decide on the *fuck it* option.

"Jessica, I was wondering something," I say.

"What were you wondering?" she asks. She's getting her voice back, but she's still staring at me.

"Would you like to come home with me right now?" I ask.

One of her girlfriends gasps and claps a hand over her mouth. Another says, "Jessica!"

She holds my eyes for a long moment, but I don't flinch. I don't look away. I show her in my gaze, in the heat of my hand on hers, that I'm completely serious.

Slowly, she stands.

"Jessica, you can't leave with him," one of her friends says.

She doesn't take her eyes off me. "You bet I can."

"Come on, you're only doing this because of Jordan."

Aha, now I see. They're out in solidarity with their recently-made-single friend. This is perfect. Revenge sex is usually fantastic.

I lean close to her so I can brush my lips close to hear ear. "After tonight," I say, pitching my voice low, "Jordan won't exist."

Her hand twitches and her mouth curls in a little smile.

"Don't worry, ladies, I'll take very good care of her," I say.

"Holy shit," one of them says under their breath.

I hold my arm out and Jessica tucks her hand in the crook of my elbow. I lead her outside, turning down the street toward my condo.

I'm well aware of what I'm doing. I don't intend to get Jessica's phone number, or be her rebound relationship after Jordan, whoever the fuck he is. I'll give her a night she'll always remember, and she'll help fill the hole in my chest—even if only for tonight.

3

KYLIE

I have to circle the block three damn times to find a parking space. I don't know why the streets around Selene's house are so clogged with cars, but it's frustrating as hell. I haven't seen her for a few weeks, but she texted me out of the blue twenty minutes ago with our code for an emergency, asking me to meet at her place. I was just leaving work, so instead of heading home I drove straight here.

I finally find a spot two blocks away and park my little Honda Civic. It's uphill to her house, and I'm in heels, so that definitely sucks. When I get to the door, I don't bother knocking, just use my key.

"Selene," I call out as I walk in the door, "where are you?"

Her muffled reply comes from the back of the house. "Couch."

I find her in the corner of the L-shaped sectional, wrapped in a thick blue blanket. Her eyes are bloodshot, her cheeks wet with tears.

"What happened?" I ask. I sink down on the couch next to her and she tips over to lay her head in my lap.

She sniffs. "Nathan..." She stops and sobs into my legs.

I run my fingers through her hair and shush her. "Oh, honey. It's okay. Tell me when you're ready."

I'm seething inside. What the hell did Nathan do to her? They seemed so happy together.

Selene sits up and wipes under her eyes. I swear, even the woman's ugly cry is pretty. She takes a deep breath. "You know how Nathan travels a lot for work?"

"Yeah."

She takes another shaky breath. "He wasn't spending those trips alone."

"What?"

"He has a woman in every city he goes to. They're, like, trip mistresses or something."

"Oh my god, Selene," I say. "What an absolute asshole."

"I know," she says.

"How did you find out?"

"He was out of town earlier this week, and he texted me something really strange, something about meeting me in the lobby," she says. "I knew, the second I got the text, that he sent it to me by mistake. Work has been so busy, I didn't think about it much for the next couple days. But he got back today, and I went over to his place so I could ask him."

"What did he say?"

Selene pulls the blanket tighter around herself. "He tried to deny it, but not very hard. At first he played it off like it was meant for a colleague, but I could tell he was lying. I asked to see his phone and he got really angry. He yelled at me, Ky—saying I was paranoid, and if I didn't trust him, maybe we shouldn't be together. I said he needed to prove I could trust him by showing me his phone. He tried to put his phone away, but I grabbed it out of his hand. For a second I thought he was going to take it back, but he just slumped down in a chair and put his face in his hands."

"Caught red-fucking-handed," I say.

"Yep," she says. "He had phone numbers, and photos ... and the texts. Fuck, Ky, he was dirty texting them on days when he and I were together."

"Oh my god," I say. "What did you do?"

"I broke his phone," she says. I see the slightest hint of a smile.

"Good girl," I say. "You should have broken his face, too."

I wrap my arms around her shoulders and draw her to me. We snuggle in on the couch, and Selene sniffs a few more times.

"I'm sorry," I say. "So what are we doing? Are we badmouthing him?"

"Definitely badmouthing."

"Fuck him, then," I say. "Dirty bastard. He should fucking die. I hope one of those bitches gives him a disease."

Selene laughs. We sit for a few minutes in silence.

"What do you need, babe?" I ask. "You hungry?"

"No," she says.

"Vodka?"

"Fuck yes."

"Good girl." I squeeze her, and she moves so I can get up.

We hit the vodka, hard. It's a weeknight, and I'm going to pay dearly for this tomorrow. But it's my duty. A girl can't shirk her duty, can she?

After who knows how many drinks, Selene and I are still sitting on the sectional—*sitting* being a relative term. Selene is spread out along one side, dressed only in a t-shirt and underwear. I have no idea when she took off her pants. I look down and realize I took my skirt off at some point, and

I'm wearing one of Braxton's old shirts. Something about that strikes me as hilarious.

"Selene, when did I change clothes?" I ask. It's hard to get the words out, because I'm laughing.

"You wanted out of your work clothes," she says. I can tell by her sleepy eyes that she's pretty tossed, but she's not slurring her words. "I grabbed you a shirt."

I smell something and look around, sniffing. "What do I smell?"

"Vodka?" Selene asks.

"No, it's something else," I say. I grab the collar of the shirt and bring it up to my face. Oh my god. It's Braxton. "This smells like him."

"Gross."

"No, it smells so good," I say. I take another deep breath with the shirt over my nose.

"God, Ky, my brother does not smell good."

There's a hitch in her voice that cuts through my buzz. I smooth down the shirt.

"Well, my love life is shit," Selene says. I'm glad she's changing the subject. "How's yours? What happened with what's his name? The one who was out of town."

I sigh. "He blew me off again."

"No."

"Yeah," I say. "We went out one more time, that weekend after Valentine's. It was fun, but it didn't go anywhere, you know? So after that, nothing. He said he'd text me, but he didn't. I texted him a week later to see what was up, and nothing. Then a few days later, he has some story about a disaster at work. He's sorry, can we hang out, blah, blah, blah. I don't know what his game is, but I'm not playing it. I told him to kiss off."

"No kidding," Selene says. "Screw that. What's wrong with all these fucking men?"

"What men?"

We both turn at the sound of Braxton's voice. I didn't hear him come in.

"Asshole men," Selene says.

His eyes move around, like he's taking in the scene. His gaze comes to rest on me and a smile tugs at the corners of his mouth. I look down and realize that not only am I wearing his shirt, I'm also not wearing any pants. I scramble to get Selene's blanket over my lap.

"What happened?" he asks.

"Nathan had a bunch of trip whores," I say.

The anger that crosses Braxton's face sends a little jolt of fear running through me. "He what?"

Selene explains what happened with Nathan. Braxton opens and closes his fists as he listens.

"But, it's fine, Braxton," Selene says, after she finishes her story. "Don't do anything. Please."

"Fuck," Braxton says, looking away. His thick chest rises and falls rapidly. "Fuck, I want to kill that guy."

"You don't need to kill anyone," Selene says. "Just come have a drink with us."

He rubs his stubbly chin, and I can see the cords in his neck straining.

"Come on, Brax, please?" Selene says. "I broke his phone and called him lots of dirty names."

"And think of it this way," I say. "Now he has to suffer, knowing he'll have to live without Selene for the rest of his worthless life."

"Thanks, babe," Selene says.

Braxton's face softens. I lean back against the cushions,

feeling a sudden wash of dizziness pass over me. I probably could have done without that last drink.

Braxton picks up my legs and sits between me and Selene, placing my feet in his lap once he sits down.

"Stupid men," Selene says. "Nathan is the literal worst. And Ky's guy flaked on her again."

"Men are assholes; you two know that, right?" Braxton says.

He grabs one of my feet and rubs the bottom with his thumbs. My eyes flutter closed, and I have to stop myself from sighing. Man, that feels good.

"You're not an asshole, Brax," Selene says, her voice sleepy.

"No, I am," he says. "I'm the worst kind."

My eyes flutter open. He's looking at me. His hands feel good on my bare feet, and I don't want him to stop. All the vodka is making it hard to keep my eyes open.

We sit in silence for a while. I feel myself drifting in and out. I try to stay awake, but it's a battle I'm definitely losing.

Braxton squeezes my foot. "You girls should get to bed."

I force my eyes open. Selene is so out she's mouth-breathing.

"Wait here," Braxton says. "I'll carry her upstairs and come back for you."

I giggle. "Will you carry me upstairs too?"

"Your room is down here," he says.

My eyes close again. I'm so sleepy. "You smell good. I bet your sheets smell like you."

Braxton stands abruptly, tipping my legs off the couch. I bend my knees and tuck my feet under the blanket. Who needs a bed? I'll just sleep here.

Braxton's hands slipping beneath me wake me from a vivid dream.

"Where? What?"

"Shh," Braxton says, his voice throaty and low. "I'll get you to bed."

I wrap my arms around his neck and rest my head against his chest. He carries me across the living room, past the kitchen, and through my bedroom door. His chest is solid, his arms hot steel around me. My eyes don't want to stay open, but a part of me wants to wake up. To see Braxton holding me like this. To be aware of what's happening.

I feel the mattress beneath me as he sets me down. He pulls the covers up, and a second later I can tell he turned off the light. Everything melts away, floating on a sea of vodka.

"Night, Brax," I say, without opening my eyes.

"Night, baby girl," he says.

Something he said catches in my mind. "Brax?"

"Yeah?"

"You're not an asshole," I say. "You're the only one of them who isn't."

He doesn't reply and I feel myself drifting off again, the soft blankets warming me.

"I am, Ky," he says, and his voice startles me. "I really am."

The door clicks shut and I fall asleep, wondering what he means ... and wishing he had stayed.

4

BRAXTON

I grab a towel and wipe the sweat off my forehead. ACDC blasts from the speakers. It's six-thirty in the morning, but my gym is in an industrial area, so I don't have to worry about bothering the neighbors. I'm not always in at this hour, but today I have a client at seven, and I'm booked up until the afternoon. I needed to get my workout in early.

My legs burn from doing heavy squats. I walk around to loosen them up before my next set. I'm too hot, so I pull off my shirt and toss it on the floor. It feels good to get some of my aggression out. Working out has always been a must for me. It doesn't matter what else is going on—unless I'm injured or sick, I hit the gym. Hell, sometimes even when I *am* injured or sick.

Sweat runs down my chest and back, but my head clears as I do another set. It's like getting an extra hit of oxygen. I finish my workout, grab some water, and jump in the shower before my first client is due to show up. And Derek Marshall wants to stop by and take a look at the facilities again. If this guy keeps being such a prima donna, I'm going to tell him to fuck off. He won't be the last football player I have a chance to take on. But that's the thing with training pro athletes: they sign these big contracts for huge money, and everyone treats them like their dick is made of fucking gold.

Everybody except me. They pay me for results, and that's what I give them—but they have to be willing to put in the work. Most of them are. They don't get where they are by being lazy asses. But I also don't put up with bullshit excuses—whining, showing up late, or canceling appointments. If they want me to take them to the next level in their career, I'll fucking do it. But I don't put up with divas who aren't willing to work their ass off in my gym.

Does it mean I lose clients? Yeah, all the time. But I'm in high enough demand that they come to me, not the other way around. I have no problem filling my schedule. So if Derek Marshall wants to be a pussy and find a trainer who's going to coddle him, he's welcome to.

The first part of my day goes fast. I go from one client to the next, take a quick break for lunch, and see two more in the afternoon. Derek Marshall does stop by—sans manager, which is a nice change. When he's not with his entourage, he's a decent guy. He signs the training agreement, and I get him on the schedule for next week.

With that wrapped up, I head home and take another shower. I'm sweaty from training all day. Afterward, I get dressed in a pair of jeans and a dark gray shirt. It's March fifteenth, which means I have somewhere to be.

I pull up in front of the assisted living facility. It's a nice place—not the kind that smells like bleach and death when you walk in. Kylie's dad has lived here for the past year. He's only in his sixties, but a debilitating combination of rheumatoid arthritis and gout have ravaged his body. He's wheelchair-bound and has a hard time using his hands, which made it impossible for him to live alone. Kylie's parents have been divorced for years, so assisted living was the only good option. I made sure we found him a place where he'd be well taken care of, and not feel like he's doomed to spend the rest of his life in a hospital. This place was a good choice.

Chelsea at the front desk says hi when I sign in. Most of the staff knows me. I try to come visit Mr. Winters once a week, although it doesn't always work if I get busy. But today is his birthday, so there's no way I'd miss it.

I take the elevator upstairs to the top floor. He can't get out much, so I made sure his apartment had a great view. I knock and he buzzes me in.

"Hey, Mr. Winters," I say. He's told me numerous times to call him Henry, but I never do. It doesn't feel right.

"Braxton," he says with a smile. He's sitting in his wheelchair, near the living room window. With obvious struggle, he lifts a finger to press the button on the remote that's attached to his chair. The TV turns off.

I pull a bottle of Jameson from beneath my jacket and hold it up so he can see. It's not fancy, but it's what I get him every year. "Should I pour?" I ask.

"Only if you're having one with me," he says.

"I will not say no to that," I say.

I head into his small kitchen, find two highball glasses, and pour us each a drink. I stick a plastic straw in his. It looks sort of odd, like suddenly it's apple juice instead of whiskey, but he has an easier time drinking if he doesn't have to hold the glass.

He moves his chair over to the small table on the other side of the room. His hands are curled, like awkward claws, and I can see the pain in his face as he works his motorized chair. It kills me to see him like this.

I take a seat and put the drink on his tray once he's settled in place. "Happy birthday," I say, lifting my glass.

He nods to me and sips through the straw. "Strictly speaking, I'm not supposed to have this."

I take a sip, too. "Strictly speaking, I kept it under my coat on the way in. So if you don't say anything, I won't either."

"Good man."

Mr. Winters isn't my father, and he never tried to replace my dad. But in his own way he filled that role for me more than once when I was growing up. Most boys need a man to stand up to them when their balls drop and they think they're the shit. Henry Winters did that for me.

Of course, I kind of still think I'm the shit, but at least now I can back it up.

"How are you feeling today?" I ask.

"About the same," he says. "That's good news, at this point. How's work?"

"Busy," I say. "I signed Derek Marshall today."

"Good," he says, nodding slowly. "He made the right choice."

"We'll see if he still thinks so when I start kicking his ass next week."

"Don't kick his ass too hard," he says. "We need him healthy next season."

I chuckle. I know he's pitching me shit. "He's going to dominate next season. Just wait."

"All right, then," he says. "I expect a Super Bowl out of that kid."

"That's the goal," I say.

We talk about sports for a while. It's our usual topic. Half the time when I visit, we just sit and watch a game. He's having a harder time as his body deteriorates, and I think he gets pretty lonely. I try to keep it light, and act like we're sitting in his living room at his old house.

He finishes his drink. "You should clean this up and put the bottle away before the nurse comes," he says.

"No problem." I polish off the last of my whiskey. "Do you want me to take the bottle and bring it back next week?"

"No, I can keep the bottle in the cupboard," he says. "But the nurses will give me fewer dirty looks if I don't have it sitting out."

I grab our glasses and clean everything up. "Did Kylie come by yet?" I ask when I come back to the living room.

"She came for lunch," he says. "Brought me a cake."

I smile. "That's not surprising."

A serious look crosses his face. "How is she?"

"Didn't you say you just saw her?" I ask.

"I did," he says. "But I'm never sure if she means it when she says she's fine. I worry about my girl."

I smile at him. "Yeah, I think she's good. Last time we hung out, she seemed okay." I neglect to mention that the last time I saw her, she was passed out drunk on Selene's couch, looking ridiculously hot in nothing but my t-shirt. To be fair, she was break-up drinking with Selene, but I don't think her dad needs to hear about that.

"Is she seeing anyone?" he asks.

I shrug, keeping my face casual. I wish she would just tell her dad what's going on. I hate having to talk to him about her love life. "Not that I know of."

He's silent for a long moment, staring into space. "I hope she settles down soon."

I look over at him in surprise, not sure what to say.

"Having a daughter is a scary thing," he says, his voice

quiet. "At first, you're worried about them meeting the wrong guy. Then they get a little older, and you start to worry about them meeting the right guy." He meets my eyes. "Now, I have to face the fact that I won't be able to walk my little girl down the aisle. Hell, I don't know if I'll be around to roll her down the aisle either."

Fucking shit. I blow out a breath to get rid of the tightness in my chest. "You will be."

"I'm sorry, Braxton," he says with a shake of his head. "What about you? Any closer to settling down?"

"Not really." The thing with Jessica went on a little longer than I planned. We saw each other for a few weeks, although the sex wasn't that great. It's never really what I'm hoping for. The fling didn't amount to anything, and for once, it wasn't me who broke it off. It was a relief when she told me—saved me the trouble of having to be the asshole again. At least that's one girl who came in and out of my life who doesn't hate me.

"I hope you find the right woman someday," he says. "I'd like to see you happy."

I laugh to hide the way my throat catches. I've never admitted the truth about my feelings for Kylie to anyone, but especially not to him.

"I'd like to see all three of you happy," he continues. "You and Selene are my family, just as much as Kylie. I want you to know that."

"I know."

"I feel like maybe I should have done more for you and your sister," he says. "I could have been around more."

"I'm not sure where all this is coming from," I say, "but you don't have anything to feel bad about. Selene and I got dealt a shitty hand, but we survived. We're both reasonably healthy adults. We had Aunt Cindy to take care of us, and you were there a hell of a lot more than you're giving yourself credit for."

He lets out a heavy sigh. "Maybe you're right."

"Is something wrong?" I ask. Fuck, if he's dying or something...

"No, no," he says. "Birthdays just bring out the worst in me as I get older. I start thinking about regrets."

"Mr. Winters, you're a good man. The best I know. You were a good father to Kylie, and you did more for me and my sister than you ever needed to."

He meets my eyes and nods. I hold out a hand and he grasps mine with his bent and misshapen one. I clasp it carefully so I don't hurt him.

"Thank you, Braxton," he says.

I nod, but I'm suddenly choked up and can't quite say anything.

He clears his throat. "Enough bullshit from this old man. Just do me a favor, will you?"

"Anything."

"Keep an eye on my little girl," he says. "I know you do already, but I need to ask you anyway."

"I will, Mr. Winters," I say. "I will."

5

KYLIE

New Year's resolutions are meant to be abandoned, right? It's not just me?

I take a deep breath and smooth out my hair, trying to get my shit together. I resolved to stop partying so much, and going after the wrong guys so much. But tonight, I'm pretty much tossing it all out the window and doing both.

Hey, I made it into March. That's something. Most people quit going to their new gym by the end of January.

Music from the party blares through the bathroom door. I've had at least two too many drinks at this point, and I'm debating whether I should call it a night and stumble up to Selene's place, or pound another shot and see if I can rally. That guy ... what's his name, Dylan? He's been fun, and he was totally checking me out when I got up to use the bathroom. Plus he's mega hot. Maybe I should stick around and see if I can get lucky.

I really, really want to get lucky.

Why the fuck I'm so horny, I have no idea. I'm probably mid-cycle or something. Slow down, ovaries. You're on vacation right now, you sneaky little minxes. But chemically suppressed fertility or no, I haven't been well and truly fucked in months, and I'm looking to get laid tonight.

It has absolutely nothing to do with the copious amount of gin I've had.

Squaring my shoulders, I adjust my blue beaded necklace and pull my shirt down a little more so my boobs look better. You have to use the assets you have, and I do have fantastic boobs. I'll let Dylan put his face in them all night long, if he has a nice big cock and knows how to use it.

Wedge heels were probably not the best choice for tonight, but I manage to get back to the table without falling over. Selene is at another table, laughing with some of our other friends. Braxton was here, but I haven't seen him in a while. He probably took some dumb girl home with him already.

Wait, no, I see him near the bar, talking to a group of guys. Probably talking sports. All Braxton has to do is name-drop a few of his clients, and dudes go nuts. I almost angle myself toward him and keep walking to the bar. He's like a magnet. But Dylan catches my eye and smiles, beckoning me closer.

"Hey, gorgeous," Dylan says when I get back to the table. I don't think I know the rest of the people sitting here. They must be Dylan's friends. I don't know Dylan either, but he's here, and he's hot, and he's looking at me with just the right expression. The *I'm going to fuck you later* look.

I give him that look right back. *Yes. Yes, you are.*

He pulls me into his lap, and I put my arm around his shoulders.

Selene catches my eye from her spot at the other table. She raises her eyebrows, but Dylan says something and I burst into laughter. I'm not even sure what he said, but everyone else laughs, so I join in. Then the laughing itself seems funny, so I keep going.

I'm starting to fade and I haven't gotten another drink. I open my mouth to ask Dylan to get me one when he puts his mouth near my ear.

"Do you want to get out of here?"

"Oh god, yes," I say—at least, I think that's what I say. My head is spinning so much, it's taking a lot of effort not to fall right out of the guy's lap.

He helps me to my feet and pretty soon I'm fumbling with my key to Selene's house. We were right around the corner, and I planned on staying here anyway. I lead him inside, pulling my clothes off as we make our way to my room.

MY EYES ARE SO GRITTY I can barely open them. Holy shit, what did I do to myself last night? My head is already pounding with the hangover from hell. I shift a little, and something feels weird. I peek beneath the sheets. Yep, I'm naked. Why did I go to bed naked?

Oh no. I'm not alone, am I?

I look over my shoulder; sure enough, there he is. He's asleep next to me, eyes closed, his chest rising and falling. The night comes back to me, hazily. Lots of gin. Me sitting in his lap. He was either very funny, or I was very drunk.

At this point, I strongly suspect the latter.

I put my hand to my forehead and close my eyes. I remember now. Stumbling up the hill to Selene's house. Fumbling with the keys. My clothes are probably still strewn across the living room. We got in here, and—

Fuck, he was awful.

He slapped against me like a penguin waddling across a fucking glacier. How that's an apt metaphor for crappy sex, I have no idea, but it definitely fits. In five minutes—if I'm being generous—he was done, rolling off me with a self-satisfied groan, like he'd just done something amazing.

I can assure you, there was no amazing.

I get out of bed as quietly as I can and put on a zip-up sweatshirt that's sitting nearby. I'm achy, and it's not the *I had hard sex last night* kind. It's the *I didn't have an orgasm when I expected to* kind. Maybe I should have taken care of business myself afterward, but I think I more or less passed out at that point.

Now? I'm mildly throbbing. I figure I'll duck into the bathroom and see if I can DIY the tension away before Mr. Penguin Sex wakes up.

"Morning," he says, his voice sleepy.

I freeze, like a kid caught shoplifting. I turn and give him what I hope is a nice enough smile. I probably look like hell, but I'm definitely not seeing him again, so what the fuck do I care?

"Hi, um, bathroom," I say. "You can go whenever."

I duck into the bathroom, but there's no way I can relax enough to get off if I think he's listening. For a girl who hooked up with a random dude—I'm fairly sure his name is Dylan—last night, I'm surprisingly uptight about masturbation. I don't do it on a regular basis, saving it for times when I'm particularly tense. Like when I'm expecting a good O and don't get one.

But I can't do it if I feel pressure, or if I think someone is listening. There's a certain amount of relaxation necessary for any orgasm, self-induced or otherwise, and without that I can't make it happen. At this point, touching myself is only going to make the problem worse.

I linger in the bathroom, hoping he takes the hint and leaves. He doesn't. Apparently this guy is really clueless. Fortunately, I have a pair of yoga pants and a t-shirt in the bathroom. I give them a quick sniff—they smell decent enough—and slip them on. I'll have to deal with going commando, because I have no idea where my panties are. I only hope I didn't take those off in the living room too.

I decide ignoring him is my best plan, and come out of the bathroom. It's actually a terrible plan, but I'm hoping he gets the hint, even if he didn't before.

No one else is downstairs, for which I'm immensely grateful. I pick up our clothes, draping his on the couch in plain view of my bedroom door, so he won't have to hunt for them when he comes out. I hope Braxton didn't crash here last night. I feel like I'm doing the equivalent of the walk of shame, and he'll get way too much of a kick out of it if he's here to witness it.

The front door opens, and Selene walks in with two big coffees. "Morning, sunshine," she says. and hands me a coffee.

"I am so in love with you right now," I say. "Maybe we should just say fuck it all and become lesbians together."

"There are days when that is so tempting," she says.

I hold the coffee beneath my nose and breathe it in. My headache already feels better, just by the proximity to my only real love.

"So, did you hook up with that guy last night?" she asks.

As if on cue, the toilet flushes. My eyes widen.

Selene's lips turn up in a sly grin. "Is that Mr. Hookup in your bathroom?"

I groan. "Yes."

"Not a good hookup, then?"

"No," I say, with a sad shake of my head. "He was clumsy

and fast. I'm not even going to lie to you—I have the female equivalent of blue balls right now."

"Ugh," Selene says with a dramatic eye roll. "That's the worst. Why didn't you take care of it yourself?"

I shrug. "I was pretty drunk, and I fell asleep. Or passed out. Whatever. But fuck, Selene, I'm so uncomfortable."

Dylan comes out in nothing but his underwear. He sees Selene and gives her a grin. "Hi."

I point to the couch. "Your stuff is over there."

He makes a show of putting his clothes back on. Selene snickers and I barely stop myself from bashing my forehead on the kitchen counter. But my head already feels like it's going to explode, so I do not need to make it worse.

"So, do you want me to call you?" Dylan asks.

I open my mouth to reply, but I'm not sure what to say. I don't want him to call me—not even a little bit—but I don't think he has my number anyway. I'm trying to come up with a response that doesn't make me sound like a total bitch when the front door bangs open and Braxton strides in.

"Hey, Brax," Selene says. She sits on the couch with her coffee.

Braxton pauses and appraises Dylan. He's at least four inches taller than my unfortunate hookup, and he's blocking the way to the front door.

Dylan's eyes move from me to Braxton a few times. I try not to die of awkwardness.

"Morning, ladies," Braxton says.

How the fuck is he so chipper in the morning? Didn't he get shit-faced last night, too?

"Hi," I say, not bothering to fake morning enthusiasm any more than I faked an orgasm last night.

Braxton comes into the kitchen, walking past Dylan like

he no longer exists. He grabs my coffee and takes a sip. "You look like shit."

"Thanks," I say, making sure to sound extra sarcastic.

"I call it like I see it," he says.

"She has lady blue balls," Selene says over her shoulder.

My mouth drops open and Braxton raises his eyebrows.

"What the fuck?" Dylan says.

Braxton laughs and looks over his shoulder at Dylan. "I'd say that's your cue to go, big guy." He turns quickly to me, the slightest shadow of doubt crossing his features. He was dangerously close to breaking our unspoken pact with that comment, and I can tell he knows it.

I turn one side of my mouth up in a little smile. He bent the rule; he didn't break it. A shitty hookup doesn't need to be protected from him. I move my eyes to Dylan and nod toward the front door.

"See ya," I say.

Dylan makes a face like he might defend his manhood, but he just grabs his sweatshirt and leaves.

I groan when the front door closes, putting my hand to my forehead. "What is wrong with me? Seriously, that guy? Selene, why did you let me do that? You should have stopped me."

"You were beyond help last night," she says. "Having said that, I actually think you're right. I shouldn't have let that go down. It's not like you got anything good out of the deal. Just frustration."

"You still ... frustrated?" Braxton asks, raising an eyebrow.

I feel a tingle in my belly that goes right between my legs, and the throbbing starts all over again. I look away. "I'm fine."

"Just go deal with it," Selene says. "I'll turn on the TV so we won't hear if you make noise."

"God, Selene, really?" I ask. "I'm not going to go *deal with it* with you guys sitting out here."

Selene laughs. "Oh come on, it's us. Have any of us not heard the others having sex at some point? I can deal. And Braxton's my brother, so it's really gross."

"You haven't heard me having sex," Braxton says.

"Um, are you joking?" she asks. "Of course I have."

"When?"

"Too many times to count," she says. "It started back in high school. You brought that one girl home constantly."

Braxton laughs. "Nothing in our teens counts. Teenagers are bumbling idiots." He flashes a grin at me. "Well, I wasn't. But I was noisier than I needed to be."

I roll my eyes at him. "I'm sure you were amazing from the start."

He shrugs. "I was."

Somehow I don't doubt it.

"I realize I kind of brought it up, but can we stop talking about Braxton and sex?" Selene asks.

Braxton sits on a bar stool and takes another sip of my coffee, then hands it back to me. "Why? I rather like talking about me and sex."

"If you don't stop, I'll start talking about *me* and sex," Selene says.

He glares at her. "Touché." He turns his smoldering gaze back on me. "So what about it, Ky? You need me to relieve some tension? I bet I can do it in under ten seconds flat." He licks his lips and twitches his fingers.

My breath catches a little. I take a sip of coffee to cover the sudden shiver that runs down my spine. "No, I'm good."

"You sure?" he says with a smirk.

He holds my gaze for a long moment, and I'd be lying if I said I'm not tempted. A tiny bit tempted. But only because I'm so keyed up and I'm pretty sure he can make good on that ten seconds flat promise.

Then Selene's face catches my eye. She's looking at Braxton the way Braxton's last girlfriend looked at me. Murder glare.

I see the instant he realizes how his sister is looking at him. The mischievous, seductive grin is gone, as if it had never been there, and he takes my coffee out of my hands. "You really need to pick better one night stands, Ky. This is getting embarrassing."

I let out another sigh. He takes a drink and hands it back. He's more right than he knows.

"You know what, my new year's resolutions got fucked all to hell, so I'm regrouping right now," I say. "No more stupid hookups. No more pointless sex. I'm either going to be with a guy with actual potential, or no one at all."

"Good for you, babe," Selene says.

Braxton looks at me, his expression unreadable. I hate it when he looks at me like that. I don't know what he's thinking, but it usually means he's about to make fun of me.

"Yeah, good," he says. "You should be with someone with potential."

I raise my eyebrows at him. Really? That's all he's got? "Okay, then. We're all in agreement. I need you guys to help me stick with this. This year was supposed to be different, but it won't be if I keep doing the same things over and over. Isn't that, like, the definition of insanity or something?"

Braxton takes my coffee again. "Okay, then. To different." He raises the cup and takes a sip, then hands it back to me.

"To different," I say. Maybe it's not midnight on January first, but I can toast to that.

6

KYLIE

To different.

Ideas like that always sound good when you're at the beginning of them, don't they? I'm going to change! I'm going to be better! I'm going to stop jumping into bed with losers!

Six weeks into my renewed pledge to change my life, and I'm basically bored and lonely.

Other than going to work, I haven't been out much. I'm too skittish to go out, as if I won't be able to control myself and I'll let some guy's dick fall into me accidentally. I haven't had a drink since the Night of Gin and Bad Choices. I'd miss that more if I was going out, but since I'm not, it sort of works. And hey, I'm all caught up on at least five different series on Netflix, so I have that going for me.

But right now, *different* is dull.

I grab the two bags of takeout and head into the building where my dad lives, then sign in at the front desk and take the food upstairs. I Skyped Dad before I left, so he's already sitting at his little dining table when I come in.

"Hey sweetheart," he says.

I can tell right away he's having a good day. His face is relaxed and his eyes aren't tinged with pain. "Hi Dad."

I set the food on the table and get plates and silverware, hoping he can hold his fork okay. I bring everything out and dish us up. "Sorry it's been so long since I've been by," I say as I sit down. "How have you been?"

"As good as can be expected," he says.

At least he's honest. "Are you keeping busy?"

"Oh, sure," he says. "What about you? Are you dating anyone?"

Ugh, really, Dad? "No, I'm definitely not dating anyone."

"Why *definitely*?"

"I don't know," I say. "I'm focusing on me right now."

"That sounds like a bunch of magazine mumbo jumbo."

I laugh. "I just want to date the right guys instead of the wrong ones for a change."

He takes a bite. It's slow, but he manages. "You've been dating the wrong ones?"

"Well, obviously—because hi, pushing thirty and still single," I say.

Dad puts his fork down. "You'll find him, sweetheart. You just make sure he's good to you. You're a bright, beautiful woman, and you don't deserve anything less than a man who treats you well."

A lump rises in my throat. "Aw, Dad, you're going to make me cry."

He just smiles at me.

I'm not used to him being quite so ... emotive. He's usually lawyer-serious.

"So, does this working-on-you plan include finding a new job?" he asks.

I do my best not to groan. My career choice is a sore subject between us. He wanted me to go to law school.

Instead, I went to art school and got a degree in graphic design—which I have yet to actually use, because I couldn't find a graphic design job for the first few years out of college. Since then, I've more or less stopped looking.

"Work is fine," I say. That's not even a tiny bit true. My job is stupid and boring. "But I've been thinking about doing some freelance stuff."

He looks skeptical. "Well, that's something."

I try not to let him get to me. I'm holding my own, supporting myself. That's not failure, right? Just because I don't have my dream career, doesn't mean I should have gone to law school.

But I don't want to argue with my dad. We did enough of that years ago. So I change the subject and ask about his favorite sports teams. It's a surefire way to keep him talking, and away from sensitive subjects.

We finish our meal, and I clean up. I can tell he's worn out, so I say my goodbyes and leave him to get some rest.

I check my phone on my way out to my car, and find a text from Selene. It simply says, *Carrot cake.*

I text her back. *I'm there.*

I head over to Selene's house. She has a cake sitting out on a plate on the kitchen counter. It's covered in cream cheese frosting with little icing carrots all around the edge.

"Did you bake?" I ask with disbelief.

She laughs. "No, I just put it on a plate so it would look pretty. I got it from Metro Market."

"Ooh, they have the best bakery," I say. "Have you been alone all day?"

"No." There's a wickedness to her tone.

"Selene," I say. "What's up?"

She cuts two thick slices of cake and plates them. "Okay, I have a confession, which is mostly why I bought you cake."

"A confession?"

She pushes the plate toward me and hands me a fork. "I've been seeing someone for the last month and I didn't tell you."

My jaw drops. "What the fuck?"

"I know." She takes my fork from my hand and cuts a bite. "Here, eat. Yes, I kept it from you, but it's not because I didn't want to tell you. I just ... I wanted to see if it was going somewhere first."

I narrow my eyes at her, but put the bite of cake in my mouth. Oh my god, it's divine. "Okay, I'm kind of forgiving you right now." I finish the bite, closing my eyes in ecstasy as the cream cheese frosting melts in my mouth. "So, you're telling me. Does that mean it is going somewhere?"

"I think so," she says. "At least, enough that you'll meet him soon."

I take another bite. "That's awesome, babe. I'm excited. Who is he? What's he like?"

"His name is Matthew. Isn't that a great name? He's tall, of course, because that's a must for me, and he played college basketball."

"Where did you meet this guy? At work?"

"No," she says, her voice emphatic. "You know I don't date people I work with. I met him online, if you can believe it."

"I can believe it," I say. "I'm happy for you."

"Are you?"

"Yeah, why?" I narrow my eyes at her. "Is there something wrong with him you haven't told me yet?"

"No, nothing like that," she says. "I was just worried you'd be pissed that I didn't tell you about every date."

I wave my hand at her as I take another bite. "No, that's silly. It makes sense. Now I can be excited for you because you've already been through the whole *do we have chemistry and is there going to be a third date* stuff."

"Exactly," she says. "And Ky, we have chemistry. Fuckloads of it."

Is it weird that hearing her say that, with her voice lowered and kind of breathy, makes me a little tingly? I shift on the barstool, trying to get rid of the feeling. Just because Selene has a guy to give her orgasms and I don't, does not mean I need to be jealous.

"I mean, holy shit, we spent today together and, damn," she says. "He is hot, and he is good."

Okay, I'm a little jealous. "You get him, tiger," I say, and assuage my envy with more cake.

"So how's the *vow to be different* plan coming?" she asks.

I drop my fork. "I have no idea what I'm doing. I'm not dating the wrong guy, but I'm not dating anyone. I'm not even trying. I have no idea where to even start."

"You could try online."

"I guess," I say. "I'm just not sure what I'm looking for anymore. It's like my radar is broken or something. But whatever, I don't want to talk about my desolate love life. Where's Braxton? He would love this cake."

Selene licks some frosting off her fork. "I don't know. Probably with Aubrey."

My back stiffens. I haven't heard this name in connection with Brax before. "Uh, who's Aubrey?"

"You haven't met Aubrey?" she asks. "Right, I guess you've been in seclusion. They've been dating for, I don't know, a month? She's pretty nice. Different than the girls he usually dates."

Different. We both toasted to it. My tummy does a little tumble, and suddenly the cake doesn't taste like anything.

Why do I care? Braxton dates lots of girls. I shouldn't ask

more questions about her, but I can't help it. "What's so different about her?"

"She's not a blonde, for one," Selene says. "And, I don't know … she's nice, and please don't hit me for saying this, but she's not slutty. Because let's be honest, a lot of Braxton's girlfriends are kind of slutty."

A not-slutty non-blonde? I take another tasteless bite of cake to cover the fact that I feel like I got punched in the gut. But that's stupid, because I have no reason to feel this way.

I know what it is. I'm bummed because both my besties are in relationships and I'm the odd one out. That's definitely the reason this news is hitting me so hard.

"That's cool, I guess," I say. "I won't get too excited, though. It's not like she'll be around for long."

"I don't know," Selene says. "Like I said, this one seems different. He seems different with her."

I push my plate away. I need to quit shoving cake in my mouth, and I really need to change the subject. "I have got to quit eating this, or I'll definitely regret it later. It's so good, though."

"I know," she says. "You should take half of the leftovers home with you so I don't eat it all myself."

Why don't you just invite Braxton and his different *new girlfriend and let them lick it off each other's fingers?*

Fuck, Kylie, calm your shit down.

"Hell no, you are not pawning that plate of sinful temptation off on me," I say. "Toss it if you don't want to eat it."

She picks up her phone. "I'll just text Brax."

It's the weirdest thing, but the thought of seeing Braxton right now makes my stomach do another flip-flop—and it isn't the good kind.

"Sounds good," I say. "But hey, I have to get to work early

in the morning, so I'm going to head home. Thanks for the cake. Let me know when I get to meet your new guy."

She smiles. "You bet. Thanks for coming over."

I head out to my car, hurrying just in case Braxton is close by. I don't want to deal with seeing him with this Aubrey chick. Not right now. If it lasts between them, I'll have to meet her eventually. I don't know why that thought makes me feel so sick. It must be the cake. I ate it too fast.

It can't be because I'm upset that Braxton is with someone. That thought doesn't even make sense.

7

BRAXTON

When Kylie and I toasted *to different*, something shook loose inside me.

I've been living my life this way for years, doing the same things over and over. Why am I surprised at getting the same result? Maybe it's time I accept that Kylie and I aren't going to happen. I'd like to blame it all on bad timing, but I know the truth is deeper than that. We've been friends so long that it makes any change in our relationship complicated. Risky.

Plus I have no idea what Selene would do if I got together with Kylie. I see how she looks at me when I look at Ky. She does *not* like it. And that presents a problem.

If I want something other than meaningless sex and relationships that don't last, I need to be the one to change. So, like Kylie, I'm trying something different.

That's where Aubrey came in. I did not pick her up at a bar. I did not sleep with her the first time we met. Okay, I did the second time, but that's different for me. She's not my typical fling. She's petite, with brown hair cut short in a sporty bob and a smattering of freckles across her nose and cheeks. I met her in a fucking grocery store of all places, and she hit on me first.

All different. Which is why I'm giving it a real shot.

It's Friday night, and we pull up to Brody's Brewhouse. It used to be one of our favorite hangouts, but it's been a while since I've met up with Selene and Kylie here. Aubrey is dressed in a short-sleeved black shirt that shows off her toned arms, and a polka-dotted miniskirt. We head inside and find Selene already at a table. Her new guy, Matthew, sits across from her.

I wouldn't say I'm nervous as I lead Aubrey to the table, but I do have an extra kick of adrenaline running through my system. It's the first time I'll see Kylie since I started dating Aubrey. Kylie's not here yet, but she's supposed to come, and I'm not sure how this is all going to go down.

It shouldn't be a big deal, but I already feel guilty that Ky's going to be here without a date and both Selene and I brought someone. It's not the first time this has happened, with someone being the odd person out. And it's certainly not the first time I've introduced Kylie to another woman. But this time feels ... different. Like maybe I'm closing a door for real this time.

That hits me in the gut, but I push the feeling aside.

"Hey, you two," Selene says when we get to the table.

We make the round of introductions. I've met Matthew once before. I eye him with open suspicion. There's something about him that rubs me wrong. I can't put my finger on it. Maybe it's because he was an athlete. I don't like it when my sister dates athletes; they're too much like me, but she's drawn to them like a fucking bee to a flower.

After getting settled at the table and ordering drinks, we start the customary small talk—what we do, where we're from, that sort of thing. Matthew is from Texas originally, and he played college basketball; a knee injury kept him from going pro. At least that's what he claims. I'm wondering if he just didn't get drafted, and the knee injury is his story to make him sound better than he is. Aubrey grew up in California, but went to college in Seattle and decided to stay.

I'm turned at an angle so I can't see the front door without moving. I force myself not to look too many times. Is Kylie coming? I wonder if it will raise Aubrey's defenses if I ask Selene. I told Aubrey she'd be meeting my best friend, and I told her about Kylie. She just smiled and said she was excited to meet her. I wonder how long that friendliness will last, but it's kind of a moot point—at least for tonight, if Kylie doesn't show. I check my phone, but I don't have any texts. Not that I'd expect Kylie to text me tonight. She and I haven't talked much recently, and Selene made the plans for tonight. Still, I'm disappointed.

Appetizers arrive, and Selene doesn't say anything about Kylie. I get caught up in a conversation with Matthew about the ins and outs of Seattle losing the Sonics, while Selene and Aubrey chat. The food here is great; I resolve to come back more often, even if just for the homemade potato chips and beer.

I know the second she walks in. I'm not even looking at the front door. I feel it. The hair on my arms raise and the back of my neck tingles. Selene smiles and waves. I slam my walls up around me, hard. Nothing is getting through tonight.

Kylie comes to the table and pauses, her hand on the empty chair. Fucking hell, she's beautiful. Her hair is down in loose waves around her face, and she's dressed in an ass-hugging pair of jeans and an aqua blue top. The color makes her eyes more blue than gray, standing out against her pale skin.

"Hey, you guys," she says with an easy smile. "Sorry I'm late. Work, you know?"

"No problem, babe," Selene says. "We haven't ordered dinner yet."

Kylie puts her purse over the back of the chair and takes her seat. I swallow hard, trying to get my shit under control. This is not the first time I've introduced her to a girl, so why are the words suddenly dying in my throat? She looks at me expectantly—and then the weirdest thing happens.

"Hi," Aubrey says, her voice friendly. She reaches out her hand to Kylie. "I'm Aubrey. It's so nice to meet you. Braxton has told me so much, I feel like I already know you. I hope that's not weird."

Kylie looks a little stunned, but she recovers quickly, shaking hands with Aubrey. "It's really nice to meet you too, Aubrey."

Aubrey starts asking Kylie questions, her tone light. There's no hint of jealousy on her face. No sign that she's uncomfortable with meeting this woman, who I've made clear is an important part of my life.

What the hell?

This has literally never happened before. Aubrey chats with Kylie and Selene all through dinner, treating both of them like new friends. Kylie seems relaxed. She laughs and talks. That's weird, too. She's usually closed off toward my dates—nice, even chatty at times, but always reserved. Granted, my dates aren't usually this friendly toward her, so maybe that's the difference. Kylie is simply following Aubrey's lead.

Or maybe Ky is actually happy that I'm with Aubrey.

A very disturbing realization comes to me. I liked the

fact that the women I date are uncomfortable with Kylie. It was like my secret trap door. I could always fall back on my girlfriend not getting along with my best friend as an out. Kylie isn't going anywhere, so if the girl I'm dating can't handle that, it's an easy excuse to end things and move on.

I'd never thought about it that way before this moment, and I'm not sure how to feel about it now that I know.

I'm also not sure how I feel about the fact that my new girlfriend and Kylie seem to be getting along fabulously.

I'm feeling out of control, and I do not like it. I don't do *out of control*, especially when Selene is watching. I take a long pull from my beer.

This is what I wanted, isn't it? Dating someone for real, without an end game already forming in the back of my mind. Seeing my date get along with Kylie, like we could all hang out regularly and it wouldn't be awkward. Knowing that Kylie will sooner or later not show up to Friday night dinner and drinks alone. She'll be with someone new, and he could be different, too. He could be the one who does it right. Who treats her the way she deserves, and gives her what she needs. This is what moving on looks like. What it feels like.

It feels kind of fucking awful.

But I don't let an ounce of that show. I put a hand on Aubrey's thigh. I smile at Selene. I laugh when Matthew makes a shitty joke. I can't quite look at Kylie, but I try to hide that, too.

I keep it casual. Easy. Like this night is nothing more than a bunch of friends hanging out, having a few beers.

Because that's what it fucking needs to be.

8

KYLIE

I don't want to admit it, even to myself, but I've been avoiding Braxton and Selene.

Whenever they want to hang out, I'm quick to make an excuse: I'm tired from a long week at work, I need to go visit my dad, I'm going to chill at home. I can tell Selene is annoyed with me. Her texts keep getting shorter. I feel bad, and I've almost apologized at least ten times. But every time I try to say *sorry I haven't been around lately*, I come to the part where I explain why, and I can't.

I've been the odd woman out before. That's usually mildly annoying, but it's never stopped me from hanging out with them. I might decline a group dinner, but meet up with them for drinks another time. Or find ways to hang out with them without their dates. But lately, I just can't do it.

I don't understand why. What kind of person can't be happy for their friends when their friends are happy? That's all kinds of fucked up. Selene and her new guy are getting along well, and Braxton seems like he's actually found someone outside the tall, blond, resting-bitch-face mold.

Aubrey didn't even seem like she hated me, which was weird as hell. I should be glad for them.

But I'm not.

I know I should stop telling myself this is about both of them. If it was just Selene, I'd have no issues. I am glad for Selene, genuinely.

Which means it's about Braxton, and I do not want to explore what *that* means for me.

So I keep making excuses and avoiding the entire situation. Great plan, right? Real grown up of me.

But today, I can't make an excuse and I can't ignore them. It's Mother's Day, and the three of us have a tradition to keep.

I don't particularly like Mother's Day. Both parental holidays are tough on Selene and Braxton, so that's certainly a part of it. But whereas Father's Day just means the three of us hang out with my dad, Mother's Day is tough on me, too. Talking about my mother still doesn't come easily to me. I haven't spoken to her in years. She left my dad for another man when I was little. Moved off to California and started a new family, leaving Dad and me behind. I didn't see her much as a kid, other than the two weeks I was forced to stay with her every summer—until I was thirteen and refused to go.

I didn't get in trouble for that act of rebellion. There was no coaxing or cajoling me to get in the car and drive to the airport. Dad acted upset, then had a phone conversation with my mother behind a closed door. And I never went to California to stay with her again.

It's more or less impossible not to feel pretty fucking abandoned when your mother leaves you. What was so wrong with me that she didn't want me? It wasn't that she didn't want kids; she had three more. I looked her up on

Facebook once, a few years ago, and her feed was full of posts about my half-siblings. Bragging about their accomplishments, posting pictures of them all together. What a fucking shit show. I blocked her, even though she's never made any attempt to contact me.

So with Selene and Braxton's mom gone, and mine being the unloving narcissist that she is, we've always spent Mother's Day together. It's just what we do.

I head over to Braxton's gym where we're meeting up. There are a couple of cars parked out front—Braxton's being one of them—but no sign of Selene. I consider waiting in the car until she shows up. This isn't a bring a date sort of day, so I'm positive Aubrey isn't here, but I can't decide if that's a good thing or a bad thing. I don't like the idea of being alone with Brax right now.

I blow out a long breath. This is stupid. I'm building this up in my mind so much that I'm all worked up over nothing. I'll see Braxton, and it will be the same as it always is. We'll go do our weird little Mother's Day ritual: a ferry ride from Seattle to Bainbridge and back, then dinner at this little hole-in-the-wall Mexican place in Belltown, before we go visit their parents' grave sites. I can totally handle it.

I walk in the front door and find Braxton putting equipment away on the other side of the gym. The sight of him hits me like a train; my lungs go empty like he's just sucked all the oxygen out of room. Burned it up with the heat of his body.

He gives me an easy smile and I do my best to smile back.

See? This is fine. Completely normal.

"Hey, baby girl," he says, as he saunters over to me. "How are you? I haven't seen you in a while."

I lift one shoulder. "I'm good. Same. How about you?"

He nods. "Good. Same."

We both pause and I hate the fact that I feel awkward around him.

"So, did you have a client this morning?" I ask.

"Yeah, finished up a little bit ago," he says. "So hey, I've been meaning to ask you—have you started the freelance thing yet?"

"I actually put a website together," I say, "and I'm looking into a few options for finding clients, but I haven't decided on a direction yet."

His eyes light up, and I'd be lying if I say it doesn't make me feel damn good to see him look proud of me. "That's awesome," he says. "I actually think I have your first client for you."

"Really? Who?"

"Me."

"What?" I ask. "You?"

"Yeah, the gym needs a new logo," he says. "I don't know why I didn't have you do it originally. I have this generic thing I use now, but I want to get new signage made, maybe t-shirts and stuff. What do you say? Can I hire you?"

I hesitate for a second. Is there anything wrong with this setup? Any reason I should say no? I'd love to design his logo. The thought of tapping into my creative side again is exciting. And it would give me something real to add to my portfolio—something other than mockups and old school projects.

"I'd love to," I say.

He smiles—that ridiculous brain-melting smile of his—and I fight back the temptation to hug him.

"Great," he says. "We can talk more about it later. I need to go shower. Selene's running late anyway, and she'll bitch if I smell."

I think he smells heavenly, even from several feet away, but I shove that thought away as fast as I think it.

His phone buzzes and he pulls it out of his pocket. A smile crosses his lips, and my back clenches. I'll bet anything it's Aubrey.

He pockets the phone and smiles again. "Shower. I'll be right back."

I close my eyes and shake my head while he walks away.

The door opens behind me and I inadvertently gasp when a man as tall as Braxton walks in the door. I recognize him instantly—Derek Marshall.

I've seen him on TV, so seeing him in person is a trip. He definitely looks like a football player. He's wearing shorts and an Under Armour compression tank that shows off every line of muscle he has. And he has plenty—all of them, in fact.

He smiles at me, and I feel my heart flutter a little.

"Hi," he says. "Sorry, I forgot my wallet in the locker room."

"Oh, sure," I say. "I think Braxton is in there, but I'm sure he'll be out soon."

"Right." His eyes don't leave my face and he holds out a hand. "Derek."

"Yeah," I say. "Of course you are."

He takes my hand in his much larger one. "And you are?"

"Oh, sorry," I say, flustered. "Kylie. Kylie Winters."

"It's nice to meet you, Kylie," he says. "Are you ... here to see Braxton?"

There's something in his voice. Oh my god, is he asking me if I'm *with* Braxton? "Yeah, he's an old friend."

"But not boyfriend?" he asks.

Wow, a little bold. I like that.

I laugh. "Oh god, no. Braxton and I have known each other since we were kids. He has a girlfriend. Who isn't me."

One corner of Derek's mouth turns up. "Interesting. So, what about you? Braxton isn't your boyfriend, but is someone else?"

I brush my hair back from my face. I'm feeling a little warm. "No, no boyfriend."

"That is very surprising," he says.

"I don't know about that," I say.

Derek steps a little closer. "Since I don't seem to have any competition at the moment, I think I should take advantage. Would you like to go out sometime?"

My mouth opens, but it takes me a second to gather my wits. They seem to have scattered. Did Derek Marshall just ask me out? "I'd love to."

His smile widens as he pulls out his phone. "How about Tuesday? Give me your number and I'll text you."

"Tuesday is great," I say. *Holy shit!* We exchange numbers and he puts his phone away.

"Hey, Derek, what's up?" Braxton's voice makes me jump.

"Hey, man, I think I left my wallet," Derek says as he walks to the back. "I'll just run in and see if it's there."

Braxton looks at me funny. Did he see Derek and me exchange numbers? Does he care?

He fucking shouldn't.

Derek is back before either of us says anything. He pauses at the door and looks back at me. "It was great to meet you, Kylie. I'll text you about Tuesday."

"Looking forward to it," I say.

"What was that about?" Braxton asks after the door closes.

"Nothing," I say. "He asked me out."

Braxton raises his eyebrows. "He asked you out?"

"Is that so shocking?" I ask. "What, does he usually date supermodels and you can't fathom why he'd be interested in me?"

He looks away. "No, that's a dumbass thing to say, Ky. I'm just surprised you said yes."

"Why?" I ask.

"I don't know."

I draw my eyebrows in and put a hand on my hip. "Is there a problem?"

Braxton opens his mouth to answer but Selene bursts in.

"Hey, you guys, I'm so sorry I'm late. My team had a working retreat yesterday, and I'm still getting messages from my boss," she says. "Apparently he doesn't give a shit that it's Sunday."

My phone vibrates and I check it as we walk to Braxton's car.

Hey, it's Derek. Just making sure you gave me your real number.

I smile. *If you're the good looking tall guy I just met at a gym, then yes, I gave you my real number.*

Perfect. Figured I'd check before I start sending sexually charged texts. That could get awkward.

Okay, I like this guy. *Now I'm even more excited for Tuesday.*

Me too, Kylie. Me too.

9

KYLIE

I wish I knew why Selene is so obsessed with the triple date concept. It's like this big must-do thing for her when we're all dating people at the same time. She won't let it go until Braxton and I agree. I guess she wants to make sure we can all still hang out together—that the people we date mesh well enough that we can be in a group and not have it completely crash and burn.

About half the time, it's fun, usually when our semi-awkward group of six drinks enough. Other times, awkward wins and it usually heralds the end for at least one of our relationships.

This time? I'm not even sure what to think.

I'm meeting everyone at Brody's, which feels weird since the last time I was here I met Aubrey for the first time. But today I'm not coming alone.

Derek is kind of awesome. I admit I'm a teensy bit star-struck, since he's sort of famous, but when we're together he's pretty down to Earth. And there's nothing quite like a guy who pursues you. I had to change our first date from a Tuesday to Thursday because of work, and he spent the days in between sending me a variety of sweet and sexy texts. It wasn't annoying or invasive. It was fun and flirty, and I did *not* mind the attention.

We hit it off right away and have spent quite a bit of time together. His schedule is pretty open, since it's the off season, so we hang out a lot. He's even been talking to me about how things will change when he goes back to work. That means he's thinking about the future, even if that isn't too far down the road.

Different. A guy with potential. Fun. Sexy. He checks all the right boxes. This is definitely a good thing.

I pointedly ignore the fact that I have to tell myself *this is a good thing* way too often.

I was caught up at work late, mostly because I've been sneaking off and working on design projects during work hours. Which is shitty of me as an employee, but I'm kind of over it. My admin assistant job is not where I want to be five years from now—hell, even a year from now. The thought of quitting to go full time as a freelancer is scary as shit, but I've decided it's my goal. Since I started working on Braxton's logo, I've put myself out there a little more and picked up a couple of new clients. It's pretty exciting.

My year of change is finally starting to come together.

Everyone is already at the table when I get there, even Derek. Matthew's looking at him kind of wide-eyed, like he can't quite believe he's sitting in the presence of a pro football player.

I'm not going to lie, that makes me preen a little bit.

"Hey, you guys," I say as I take a seat next to Derek, "sorry I'm late." A waitress comes and passes out drinks, including a tall glass of Red Hook for me. I turn to Derek. "Thanks."

"Yeah, Braxton ordered for you," Derek says, and takes a drink of his beer.

"Thanks, Brax," I say.

Braxton lifts his glass, and I clink mine against his.

Food comes out, and we all have a few beers. The conversation is easy and relaxed. The guys talk sports. Us girls talk about random things—work, how Selene is addicted to some show and can't wait for the next season. She and Aubrey seem to get along great, and for once Braxton is dating someone who doesn't shoot daggers out of her eyes when she looks at me.

The meal winds down; Selene looks ecstatic. It's been pretty much the perfect triple date, and I know she's utterly joyous over it. It feels a little weird that I've barely spoken to Derek through the whole meal, but I chalk it up to all the sex-segregated talk at the table tonight.

"Hey, you guys," Aubrey says, out of the blue, as we're dusting off a plate of fresh cinnamon sugar donuts. "I have an idea. My family has a vacation rental over in Leavenworth. What if we all went? It's a four bedroom, so we'd have plenty of space, and all we need to pay is the cleaning fee. What do you guys think?"

"Oh my god," Selene says. "I love this idea."

I glance at Derek, wondering how he feels about it. He can't be interested, right?

"Sounds great," he says. "As long as it's before training camp starts, I'm in." He smiles at me and puts a hand on my thigh.

I force a smile. Why am I so hesitant about this? I have to admit, we had a pretty fun dinner, all six of us. There are worse things than spending a weekend with friends. And a little time away with Derek would give us a chance to get to know each other better before he gets busy with football season.

"Yeah, sure," I say.

"Awesome," Aubrey says. "I'm pretty sure they had a cancellation a few weeks from now, but I'll text everyone to confirm."

I look down at my plate and pick at my donut. I swear I feel Braxton's eyes on me. I look up and, sure enough, he's watching me. What is he thinking? I wish I could fucking read his face. I've known him just shy of forever, and he still has the ability to hide everything from me.

I glance away. I don't trust myself to meet his eyes when he's looking at me like that.

My phone rings, startling me awake. I suck in a quick breath and grab it, noting that it's one in the morning.

It's Braxton.

"Braxton, what's wrong?" I say, trying to not sound like I just woke up.

"Hey Kylie," he says. "Sorry, did I wake you?"

"Kinda."

"Sorry, it's nothing. I'll let you go back to sleep."

"No," I say quickly, before he can hang up. "No, it's okay. What's up?"

He's silent for a moment, but I can tell he's still on the other end. "Can I come over?"

"Yeah, of course," I say.

"Thanks, Ky," he says. "Be there in a few."

I drag myself out of bed, pull on some leggings, and throw a long cardigan over my tank top. I put on some hot water for tea, wondering what's going on with him. Coming over at one in the morning doesn't mean he wants to hang out. It means something is wrong.

I settle in on the couch with my tea, and it isn't long before he knocks. He lets himself in with his key. He looks a little rumpled, like he went to bed in his clothes.

He's still the most gorgeous man I've ever laid eyes on, but let's not dwell on that.

"Hey," I say, sitting up as he comes in. "What's going on?"

He sinks down on the couch next to me. "It's just been one of those days."

My chest feels tight. I know he doesn't mean work was hard, or his car broke down, or even that something happened with his girlfriend. He's missing his parents.

He stares straight ahead for a while, and I just let him sit. He'll talk when he's ready, if he wants to. He's just as likely to get up and leave without saying anything, and never mention it again. But somehow I can tell it helps him to sit here, whether he wants to talk or not. This isn't the first time.

"I didn't want to have to explain it all to her," he says after a while.

"Who?"

"Aubrey," he says. "She knows we lost them, but ... you know. You were there."

I swallow back the lump in my throat and bite my lip so my eyes don't tear up. "Yeah."

"I don't know why tonight was shit," he says, his voice low and quiet. "It's no one's birthday, or some fucking holiday. It just hits me sometimes, out of nowhere."

I so rarely see this side of Braxton. I'm never sure how to handle it when I do. Right now, I want to put my arms around him, hold his head to my chest. But I don't. I can't.

"Can I get you anything?" I ask.

He shakes his head. "Can I just sit with you for a while?"

"Yeah," I say. "Of course you can."

He looks at me, his deep dark eyes so piercing and true. "Thank you, Kylie."

That lump is back in my throat, and it's all I can do not to cry. I put my tea down on the coffee table to give myself an excuse to look away. "Anything for you, Braxton."

Anything.

10

BRAXTON

I wish Aubrey had run this *weekend away* idea by me before she blurted it out at the table. I'm not sure how I feel about the whole thing. As it is, a few weeks later I find myself walking into a vacation house in Leavenworth with her. Selene and Matthew drove in with us, and Derek and Kylie pull up about twenty minutes afterward.

Derek and Kylie.

I feel like my life is rapidly spinning out of control. I started dating Aubrey to take control back. This was my different. I was sick of the way things were—but instead of making things better, I'm pretty sure all I've done is make them worse.

If I wasn't with Aubrey, Kylie might not have met Derek.

I'm not such an asshole that I don't want Kylie to be happy. But he looks at her in a way that makes me want to punch him in the fucking face. Like she's his. He barely knows her.

Yeah, maybe someday another guy will earn the right to look at her that way, but they have to put in the work first. They don't get to date her for a month and claim her forever.

Fuck, I'm a mess.

I have to admit, the house is nice. I can see why Aubrey was so excited. It's right on the river, just a short walk from town. There's a big kitchen, four bedrooms, a couple bathrooms, and a balcony overlooking the river.

Leavenworth is pretty touristy—everything is made to look like an old Bavarian village—but the mountains are gorgeous and the weather is supposed to be perfect all weekend. We all show up late on Friday night and don't do much other than pick rooms and sack out.

I try not to wonder whether Derek and Kylie are having sex in the room on the other side of the house. Aubrey sucks me off before we go to sleep, which I admit takes my mind off everything for a little while.

That probably makes me a bad person.

The next day, the girls want to go into town and walk around. The guys get roped into it by default, although I don't know why they want us along. Selene and Kylie seem content to go without us, but Aubrey insists we all go. She says it's so we can have lunch together, but I can't shake the feeling that it's because she wants to go shopping with my credit card.

She proves me right.

We wander in and out of the shops, and it isn't long before Aubrey spots a jewelry store. She drags me inside by the arm, gasping over the selection. It's not diamonds and shit, so I don't have to worry about her hinting at engagement rings (because fuck that right in the ass). But she does find a necklace she loves, and makes some not-so-subtle hints that she'd love to have it. There's a bit of eyelash batting. I shrug and buy it for her.

I buy a lot of things for her.

In fact, the longer this relationship goes on, the more I'm

beginning to wonder whether it's me Aubrey is into, or my money—because she seems to like me, but when I buy her things she *really* likes me. I've already figured out how to ensure I get a blowjob, for example: buy her a present.

I like blowjobs as much as the next guy, but this is getting old.

The girls shop for a while longer, and I buy Aubrey a dress and a pair of sandals. Kylie shoots me a weird look, but I pretend I don't notice. We have bratwurst and beer for lunch, which is pretty damn good (and I pay for Aubrey's, of course), then head back to the house. Aubrey, Selene, and Matthew decide to take a trip to the grocery store to get supplies. Derek wants to go for a run, and I think about joining him, but my hamstring is a little twitchy this week and I don't want to pull something.

Plus I'm having a hard time dealing with Derek.

He's my client, and within the walls of my gym it's all business. I can stay focused on my job. I'm getting him ready for training camp, and like hell if I'm going to let this fucked-up storm in my head interfere with work.

Outside the gym, though, I vacillate between mild disdain and wanting to choke him out.

I decide to go sit out on the deck with a beer, relieved as fuck that Aubrey left. I already need some space from her, and the weekend isn't half over.

Kylie comes through the sliding door and stops. She's holding a beer in one hand and a book in the other. "Oh, hey. Sorry, I didn't realize anyone was out here."

"It's fine, baby girl," I say with a smile. "Come sit."

She takes the lounge chair next to mine. Her shorts show the length of her legs, and her tits look magnificent in her little tank top. I try not to stare too much.

"What?" she says.

I raise my eyebrows. "What do you mean, what?"

"Why are you looking at me?"

Shit, I'm not doing a good job of not staring. Oh well, fuck it, then. "Because you're a beautiful woman."

"Knock it off, Brax," she says.

"Knock what off?" I ask, feigning innocence.

"You know," she says.

I'm getting hard looking at her, and I do need to knock that off. It's been easier dating a girl who doesn't seem to hate Kylie, but I can't help but feel like Aubrey's hiding a vindictive streak under that smile. She's a little *too* friendly to Kylie. Too forced. If Aubrey comes back to find me sporting a hard-on while I'm alone with Ky, it might break that facade apart.

But would that be such a bad thing, really?

"What are you reading?" I ask. I *should* stop staring at her, but I don't want to stop talking to her. We've hardly seen each other over the last couple months.

"Oh, I don't know. It's just a suspense thing someone at work loaned me."

She opens the book, but I can tell from the angle of her face that she isn't reading. She's staring out at the river. I watch her from the corner of my eye, wondering what she's thinking.

I'm losing her.

The thought comes to me out of nowhere, and I get a sick feeling in my stomach. We're growing apart. In my quest to commit to a relationship, I've inadvertently pulled away from Kylie. She's pulling away from me, too—more and more each day. Is this the inevitable decline of our relationship? Am I going to wake up ten years from now, married with a couple kids, and realize I haven't talked to her in years?

I take another drink, trying to drown that thought.

"So, how are things with Aubrey?" she asks, her voice tentative.

Her question takes me completely by surprise. "Um..." I hesitate. Should I talk to her about this? What should I say? What *can* I say? "Yeah, you know, not bad."

Chicken shit.

"Good," she says. "That's good."

"Why?" I ask.

Now she looks like she's not sure what to say. "I don't know. I was just wondering."

I take a breath. "Actually, I'm not really sure how it's going." At least that's honest.

"Why not?" she asks.

This is uncharted territory for us, and I have another sudden revelation. I've always considered our unspoken pact to be something that protects *her*. But it occurs to me as I choose my words, that more than anything, I'm protecting myself. Because if we get too deep into this topic, how am I going to avoid telling her that the real reason I'm shit with women is that none of the women I'm with are her?

I wouldn't be shit with her. Fuck, I really wouldn't.

I'd be different with Kylie. I wouldn't push her away. I'd cherish her, like she deserves to be cherished. I'd let her in.

Damn it, why do I keep thinking this way? This is what I was trying to *stop* doing.

I take a deep breath. All right, if we're going to have this conversation. "There are good things about her," I say, testing the waters, "but I'm not sure if this is right for me."

"Maybe it just hasn't been long enough," she says. "Relationships take time to build."

I nod, taking a swig of beer. "Is that what you think? That I need to give it more time?"

She pauses, chewing on her bottom lip. "If she makes you happy, then yeah."

"Do you think she makes me happy?"

"Honestly, Braxton, I wouldn't know. You seem happy, I suppose."

Okay, so if she can ask, does that mean I can too? "So, how are things with Derek?"

She hesitates. I love that she hesitates. It means she has a reason, something that makes her think. "Good, I guess."

"You guess?" I ask.

"Well, yeah, it hasn't been that long," she says. "There are good things about him, too."

"But?" I ask.

"I don't know," she says. "Maybe there isn't a *but*."

"I could hear the *but*," I say.

She laughs. "Now you sound like you're trying to talk dirty again."

I raise an eyebrow and grin at her. "You want me to start talking dirty?"

She lets out an exasperated sigh. "Derek is fine. He's a good guy. He's nice to me, and he's fun to hang out with."

I pause, watching her. God, I want to fuck this woman. I want to fuck her so hard, and so good, she'll never want anyone else for the rest of her life. I want to give her every inch of me, bury myself deep inside her, show her how long I've wanted her.

"I'm not the man you think I am, Kylie." *Shit.* That's not what I meant to say.

Her eyes are on me, but I don't meet her gaze.

"What do you mean?" she asks.

I take another drink of beer. I need to adjust my dick because it's trying to stand straight up, but she doesn't look away. "I thought I was doing the right thing, but I feel like maybe I've made it all worse."

I expect her to ask what I'm talking about, but she just stares at me. "Maybe things can still be better," she says, her voice quiet.

I freeze, staring at the water. My body aches with need for her. I want to scoop her up in my arms, pull her on top of me, and kiss her until neither of us can breathe.

This is wrong.

I'm trying to do things right. Neither of us are single. I might be an unbridled asshole, but I won't be that guy.

I get up and walk inside before I do something I'll regret.

11

KYLIE

As soon as Selene gets back with groceries, I make a bee-line for the booze.

I regretted coming here the moment we arrived. I know Selene wants to turn us into a little *Friends*-esque group of three and three, but there's just no way that's happening. Despite the fact that Aubrey is nice to me, it's fake. I know it's fake. I'm not sure what her game is, but there's no sincerity about her. Not with anyone.

She's using Braxton for his money, and it pisses me the hell off. She's not the first gold digger he's attracted, but she seems more insidious than most. She hides it so well. I hope he's being careful with her, because she totally strikes me as the type to get knocked up on purpose.

I take my Solo cup—mostly rum, with a little splash of coke—and sit at the kitchen table. I haven't seen Braxton since he started talking like a fucking alien took over his body, then walked off without another word. His voice made me shiver more than usual when he said he's not the man I think he is.

What did that mean?

Derek gets back from his run, all sweaty and flushed. He takes a bottled water out of the fridge and swallows half of it in one go. "Hey, babe, I need a shower. Wanna join me?"

I probably should want to join him, but I'm not in the mood. Like, at all. I give him an apologetic smile. "I just poured a drink, and this book is so good."

He doesn't look disappointed, just shrugs. "All right. I'll be down in a bit."

I'm glad he doesn't push, but would it kill him to give a shit?

Derek is the other problem. The awkwardness between him and Braxton is impossible to ignore. At first, Derek seemed fine with Brax. I figured it was because they already knew each other. But that's changing—fast. I see the way Derek gives him the side-eye when Braxton talks to me. If he had seen Brax and I outside on the balcony earlier, I'm sure I would have heard an earful about it.

It sucks, because Derek is Braxton's client—an important one. If I can't manage to keep these two relationships from clashing, I'm worried I'm going to ruin that for Braxton. I don't want to be the reason he loses a client, but the level of hostility between them seems to be growing.

I finish off more of my drink. It burns going down and quickly spreads, making my head a little fuzzy. I decide I'd like it to be more than a little, and take another gulp. This is how I'll get through the rest of the weekend. I won't sit here brooding about how confused I am, stressing about the fact that I think Braxton is making a huge mistake with Aubrey, wondering if I'm making a huge mistake with Derek.

I'll drown all that bullshit in rum, and have a good fucking time.

My let's-party attitude is contagious, and pretty soon the drinks are flowing.

Braxton reappears, and seems to think my plan is a good one. I see him pound two shots in a row as soon as he gets to the kitchen. Aubrey, the little gold digger, changed into her new dress, and she hangs on Braxton's arm like she needs to mark him.

By the time the sun goes down, we're all drunk as shit.

Even Derek, who doesn't usually drink much, is laughing his ass off with Matthew. I have no idea what they're talking about that's so funny, but I don't really care. I've had too much rum to care about anything.

I sit on the couch, half-listening to the conversation, and realize everyone is sharing stories about losing their virginity. Selene looks a little wistful as she talks about her high school boyfriend's attempt at romance. Matthew's was in the back of a car. Derek's was after winning a big football game —because of course it was. Aubrey's was camping, and suddenly everyone is laughing at Matthew's "fucking in tents" jokes. Braxton is oddly tight-lipped about his. I'm expecting him to brag about how awesome he was from the beginning, but he just shrugs and says something about sneaking her into his bedroom.

All eyes turn to me. Oh, god. Do I really have to play this game? I don't like talking about my first time. It's not a good story.

"What about you, Kylie?" Matthew asks.

I hedge for time by taking a drink.

"It's fine, she doesn't have to answer," Selene says.

I give her a grateful smile.

"What's the big deal?" Matthew says. "It's not like it was last week."

"No, it just wasn't that great," I say.

Aubrey laughs, then meets my eyes. "Well, no one's first time is that great. Come on, Kylie. We all told ours."

My back stiffens. There's no doubt in my mind that she's challenging me. "Fine," I say. Somewhere in the back of my head I realize that if I was sober, I'd never tell this story. Not here. Not with these people who barely know me. I've never even told Braxton.

But I'm definitely not sober.

"His name was Ryder," I say. "Good-looking guy. Popular. Every girl wanted him. He took me to a school dance. Afterward, he was supposed to take me home, but instead he drove out to an abandoned lot where no one was around. I had the feeling it wasn't the first time he'd taken a girl there. I didn't really want to, but he wouldn't take no for an answer."

That's a good way to kill a buzz. Everyone stares at me in silence. I should stop talking, but rum and good choices don't mix.

"He didn't give a shit that it hurt. Or that I cried after. When it was over, he took me home, like nothing had happened. I didn't tell anyone for a long time. I just wanted to forget about it."

"Oh, Kylie," Selene says, her voice soft.

Aubrey and Matthew shift uncomfortably, but Derek and Braxton both stare at me, their faces clouded with anger. A vein sticks out on the side of Braxton's neck, and he's breathing hard.

They both start talking at the same time, and I can't tell what either of them say. They stop, turning their gazes on each other.

It's like a fucking Old West showdown on some dusty road in front of a saloon. All they need are six shooters at their hips, and one of them would wind up with a bullet hole in his chest. They stare each other down, like they're competing for who gets to be angrier on my behalf, who has the right to try to make me feel better. My shoulders clench and the tension in the room is so thick, I can barely breathe.

"Damn, that's fucked up," Matthew says, as if he's completely clueless to the fact that the two men in front of him look like they're about to hit each other.

I need to backtrack out of this. Fast. "Yeah, well, I kicked him in the nuts later, so it worked out okay."

Aubrey laughs again. "Wow, that's intense."

Derek comes over to the couch and puts a hand on my arm. "That's brutal, babe." He kisses the top of my head and walks past me toward the kitchen.

I need some air. Selene was the only person in the world who knew about that, and I just blurted it out for everyone to hear. I get up and head outside to the balcony.

The temperature has dropped significantly since the sun went down. The air has a bite to it, despite the fact that it was well over eighty earlier today. I wander out to the railing and lean against it, listening to the soothing sound of rushing water from the river below. The chill air clears my head a little, but my stomach is still in knots. It isn't from the rum, although I've definitely had too much.

I hear the sliding glass door open and close. I know who it is. I don't even have to look.

I turn, about to say that I'm fine. Before I can speak, Braxton's arms are around me, crushing me to his chest. I go stiff, tears flooding my eyes. Oh god, he feels good. He should not feel this good. His arms are thick and his body warm. He's strong and steady, and he smells like cedar and whiskey. I let my eyes drift closed, let him hold me tight, banishing the worry over what everyone will think if they look outside.

Braxton doesn't let go. I feel his chest rise and fall as he breathes, the cold air brushing across my skin a sharp contrast to his body heat.

Braxton's voice is a throaty whisper. "I wish you would have told me."

"There wasn't anything you could do," I say, "and I didn't want you to kill him and go to jail."

His arms are unrelenting. "I could have done this."

I relax against his warmth, the tension melting from my body. My arms are bent, tucked close to my sides—the only thing keeping this from being a true embrace. Braxton rubs his hands up and down my back. I want to slide my arms around his waist, pull him closer. I want to bury my face in his chest and cry. I don't know why. Enough time has passed that I'm no longer hurt over what happened. I don't like talking about it, but the memory no longer makes me sick to my stomach. But I feel the sting of tears and my throat tightens.

Derek is going to see this. It's dark, but the sliding door is right off the kitchen. What am I going to say to him? I was drunk and upset? Braxton's a good friend and I needed a hug? His arms feel like home and I don't want him to stop?

The door opens and I gasp. Braxton's arms drop and we both step away. The cold air rushes back around me, like I just walked into a bank of fog after sitting in front of a warm fire.

"Oh, hey, you guys." It's Matthew. "Kylie, Selene's looking for you. Are you okay?"

Braxton's eyes are on me. Even in the dark, I can see their intensity. My heart beats too fast.

"Yeah, I'm fine," I say, trying to sound casual. "Can you tell her I'll talk to her tomorrow? Too much rum, you know?"

"No shit. I think we're all starting to fade. See you guys in the morning."

"Night," I say.

Matthew closes the door.

Braxton doesn't move.

I don't know what I want him to do. I want his arms around me again, but I don't want Derek to see. What does that say about me?

Nothing good.

"I'm okay, Brax," I say. "I'm just drunk. I need to go to bed."

I don't wait for his reply. I head back inside and go straight to my room, leaving him standing on the balcony.

12

BRAXTON

I'm pretty sure I know what I have to do, but I decide not to do it in Leavenworth.

A week goes by, and I avoid Aubrey. I don't pick up when she calls, and I procrastinate answering her texts. I'm not just going to blow her off, but I need some time to get my fucking head on straight.

Monday afternoon I'm done training early, so I go visit Mr. Winters. It's a clear day, the breeze keeping it from being too hot. I find him out in the garden behind his building when I arrive. His nurse hovers nearby, and she gives me a nod.

"Braxton," he says. "I didn't expect to see you today."

"You mind?" I ask.

"Of course not," he says. "You're welcome anytime. You know that."

There's a bench next to him, and I take a seat. We sit in silence for a while. The sun feels good on my skin.

"So, what's going on?" he asks, breaking the silence.

I consider denying that anything is going on, but the

truth is, I came here so I could talk to him. "Do you think I'm doomed to be alone?"

Mr. Winters snorts. "I think you know my answer to that. Why? Things not working out with Aubrey?"

"No," I say. "I think I need to break things off with her."

"Are you wondering if it's the right thing to do?" he asks.

"Not really," I say. "I think she likes my money more than anything, but that's not even the real problem."

"What is the real problem?" he asks.

I almost say it. I almost tell him that I'm in love with his daughter. That I've loved her since we were kids, and it's killing me that I can't be with her.

But I don't.

"I don't love her," I say. "I like her, I suppose. She's beautiful and we have a good time. I know I haven't been with her long, but I don't see that ever changing."

"Then you're right to end it," he says. "Being with the wrong person is never a good idea."

We both go quiet for a while. I wait until his nurse goes inside, then hand him the flask I sneaked in.

He takes a pull and hands it back to me. "Love is a shit show."

I can't help but laugh. "It really is." I take a drink and put the flask on the bench next to me.

"You probably think I'm a cynic," he says. "I'm not. I can't regret marrying Kylie's mother—without her, I wouldn't have Kylie—but she was a bad decision. A series of them, if I'm being honest."

"Did you ever think about getting remarried?" I ask.

"I did," he said. "But I was always too worried about Kylie. I didn't want someone to interfere with our relationship. Plus I worked too much. I put everything I had into my practice and my daughter. I didn't have much left for someone else."

"Do you regret it?" I ask.

"A little," he says. "These days, it would be nice to have someone to share my life with. I have Kylie, and you, and even your sister. But you three have your own lives, and I want you to focus on living them."

I hand him the flask again and he takes a drink.

"Braxton, do you want me to tell you what you need to do?" he asks.

I lower my sunglasses and raise my eyebrows. "Do I?"

He hands me the flask. "You do. You're the sort of man who makes things happen. That's why you have such a successful business."

"I don't know about that. Mostly I had plenty of seed money," I say. "I could afford to take a loss for the first few years while I built up my clientele."

"True," he says. "You had a financial advantage not many young men have. But you used it well. You took hold of that opportunity and you ran with it."

I take a pull from the flask. "True."

"My point is," he says, "if there's something you want, you need to go after it. If Aubrey isn't what you want, you're better off ending it now, so at least you'll be open to what's going to make you happy."

I had the flask back to him. "You know, I think you're absolutely right."

I INVITE Aubrey over the next day so we can talk in person. It's obvious she's knows something is up as soon as she walks in. I'm usually pretty good at hiding behind my wall, but today I don't have the energy for it. I step aside when I answer the door, avoiding kissing her, and walk into the living room.

"What's going on?" she says.

I sit down on the couch. "Why don't you come sit?"

She eyes me with suspicion.

I might as well get it over with. "Aubrey, I've been thinking—"

"You're breaking up with me, aren't you?" she says. The hostility in her voice catches me off guard. Not that I expected her to be happy about it, but I wonder if she's about to loose more venom than I'm prepared for.

"Honestly? Yes."

Her eyes narrow. "You fucker."

Really? "I'm sorry, Aubrey. You're a great girl. But this isn't working for me."

"What isn't working?" she asks. "We have fun together. We have great chemistry. What the fuck else do you need?"

I need Kylie. "Look, I know you think I'm the asshole here, and usually you'd be right. But this is the least asshole thing I can possibly do for you."

"Is that supposed to make me feel better?" she asks. "Like you're doing what's best for me?"

"It's better than pretending," I say.

She gets up and wanders to the window, her arms crossed. "This is about Kylie, isn't it?"

Fuck. "What are you talking about?"

"Don't play stupid, Braxton."

I let out a breath. I don't want the first time I say this aloud to be in the middle of a breakup, but there's no point in lying to her now. "Yes. It's about Kylie."

"You know, when you told me your best friend was a woman, every alarm I have went off. You were so adamant about it, but I figured what the hell. I'd make sure you wanted me, regardless of how you felt about her. But no matter how fucking hard I worked, no matter what I did, you never looked at me the way you look at her."

"I'm sorry, Aubrey," I say. "I wanted to give us a real shot. That's the truth. But I just can't."

She grabs her purse and walks toward the door. "You're going to wind up alone, you know that, right? Because whatever crush you're nursing for her, it's never going to happen. How long have you been letting her sabotage your life? If it hasn't happened by now, it never will. Besides, who in their right mind would break up with a guy like Derek Marshall? Even you can't compete with that."

She walks out the door and slams it shut behind her.

Well, at least that was over quickly.

My first thought is to text Kylie and tell her I broke up with Aubrey. I don't think it will make a goddamn bit of difference, but I want her to know. But randomly texting her with my relationship status update might come across as odd. I don't usually make a big deal out of any break up—I just tell her the next time I see her. Maybe I'll text Selene, and make a vague Facebook post, and hope the news gets back to Kylie.

I'm surprised at how light I feel. I didn't realize how much Aubrey was weighing me down until now. Although what she said when she left still echoes through my mind. I did not like hearing that, mostly because I'm afraid it's true.

I did want to make it work with Aubrey. But living a lie isn't any better than all the shallow sex I was chasing before. It's not even that her love of my credit card was insulting—which it was. I don't love her, and it's not an issue of needing time. I won't ever love Aubrey.

There's only one woman I'll ever love.

I have no intention of going back to the womanizing I was doing before. The next time I fuck someone, it's going to be Kylie. That's simply the way it's going to be. I don't care how long I have to wait. I won't interfere with her relationship. I won't sabotage what she has with Derek, and if that goes the distance, I'll have to find a way to live with it.

But as soon as she's single, I'll be there.

13

KYLIE

Training camp and preseason start in August, and I don't see much of Derek. He has practice, and travels for games. He texts me, and we see each other when we can. I think the distance does us some good. It's good for me, anyway. I have more time to focus on the design clients I've picked up. It will still be a while before I'm earning enough to quit what I've now labeled my *day job*, but at least I'm on my way.

I go a few weeks without seeing Selene, simply because we're both busy, but she tells me over the phone that she's not so sure about Matthew anymore. She says he gets moody and ignores her. I tell her to dump his dumb ass and find someone who isn't shitty to her. I don't know if she'll listen to me.

As far as Braxton, after Leavenworth he goes totally dark. I don't see him or hear from him at all. I notice a few vague Facebook status updates that make me wonder what's going on with him, but he doesn't call.

Of course, neither do I. I'm not sure what to say to him.

Derek texts me on a Tuesday, asking if I want to get

together tonight. Five minutes later, I get the same text from Selene. I waffle a bit, trying to decide what to do, and wind up telling Selene I just heard from Derek. I suggest we all meet up somewhere. Everyone seems happy with that plan.

I head home after work to change. I'm feeling kind of saucy, so I put on a red halter top, black miniskirt, and a gorgeous new pair of black heels. They have just a hint of shimmer, plus they're high so I won't feel like such a shorty next to all the tall people I hang out with.

Derek picks me up and leads me out to the curb. I don't see his car. Instead, there's a sexy black convertible Mercedes.

"Is this yours?" I ask.

"Yep," he says, looking rather proud of himself. "I picked it up this morning."

"It's gorgeous," I say.

Derek opens the door for me and I slide into the luxurious leather seat. He gets in, puts on a pair of sunglasses, and gives me a little smile. I have a good feeling about tonight.

We arrive at the bar and find Selene, sans Matthew.

"Aw, why are you here by yourself?" I ask, as I slide into the booth across from her.

"He's sick," she says. "But I wanted to see you, so I came anyway."

"I'll go get us drinks," Derek says and heads for the bar.

I'm not sure if I want to know, but I figure I'll take advantage of Derek's absence to ask. "Is Braxton coming tonight?"

"Yeah, I talked to him earlier," she says. "I'm surprised he isn't here yet, actually."

"He's probably picking up Aubrey."

Selene's eyebrows draw down. "Aubrey? They broke up over a month ago."

My mouth drops open, and I shut it as quickly as I can. "They did?"

"Yeah," she says.

"Did she do it, or did he?" I ask.

"Oh, he did," she says. "He didn't say much about it. Just said it wasn't working out."

Holy shit. I feel like the floor just dropped out from under me. I start to stutter out a reply, but Derek comes back and hands me a beer.

"Here you go, babe," he says.

"Thanks."

Braxton walks in and saunters over to our table. He looks fucking amazing in a white t-shirt and jeans. There's nothing fancy about his clothes, but let's be honest, you don't need fancy when you have a body like that. He locks eyes with mine and his lips turn up in a smile.

Oh god, Braxton. Don't start looking at me like that tonight.

Derek puts an arm around me. He's not usually very touchy, so it feels possessive.

"Derek," Braxton says, with a nod. "Good game the other day, man. You're looking good out there." He looks from Selene to me. "How are my girls doing tonight?"

Selene shrugs. "Fine. How are you?"

"I'm good," he says, still smiling. There's a lot of enthusiasm in his voice.

"Why are you in such a good mood?" Selene asks.

"Am I?" He turns that panty-melting smile on me again. "I'm going to go get a beer."

I catch a subtle eye roll from Derek as Braxton walks away, and I let out a sigh.

Someone across the bar catches Derek's eye. "Holy shit," he says. "I'll be right back, babe. That's an old friend of mine from college." He gets up and walks over to a tall guy standing near the bar. They do the bro hug thing, complete with the over-under arms and a couple of slaps on the back.

"Is it weird that I've never met any of Derek's friends?" I ask Selene when he's out of earshot.

She glances over at him. "Kind of? Maybe he doesn't have friends here. He hasn't lived in Seattle long."

"Maybe," I say. "Family either—although I haven't introduced him to Dad, so I guess I can't complain about that. But I don't know anything about his family. He never talks about them."

"That *is* kind of odd," Selene says. She takes a sip of her martini. "Maybe he has a shitty family and he doesn't like to talk about it."

"Could be."

The weird thing is, I feel like I don't know Derek very well at all. Even after dating him for several months, there are still a million things I don't know. I have the basics—I know where he grew up, and I know a fair bit about his football career. But does he have a best friend? A favorite movie? Has he traveled other than for games? Does he want to? I keep trying to dig deeper, but he's keeping me at a distance.

Braxton returns, beer in hand, and scoots onto the bench seat next to me. His arm brushes against mine. "This is much better," he says. "I like it when I have you two to myself." He turns to me. "Hey, baby girl. It's been too long. I've missed you."

He's so close, it's hard to think. "Yeah, me too."

Selene dips her fingers in her ice water and flicks them at Braxton. "Cool it off, buddy."

"What?" he asks.

"You know what," she says.

There's an edge to her voice that makes me want to scoot away from him—although I'm not sure I can.

Braxton winks at her. "So, how's the design stuff coming, Ky?"

"Actually, I landed a new client today," I say. "It's a small app development company, but they need everything—logo, website, the works. They seem like they'll be a lot of fun to work with."

He nudges me with his arm. "That's great. I'm really proud of you."

Warmth spreads through me and I smile, basking in his approval. "Thanks, Brax."

"You know what this calls for?" he asks. "A celebration."

"Oh, come on, it's not that big of a deal," I say. "I'm still a long way from doing this full-time."

"That might be true, but we should still celebrate the little things," he says.

"Yeah, Kylie," Selene says. "You should be proud of yourself. You weren't even doing this a year ago, and now look at you."

"Exactly," Braxton says. He nudges me again. "I'll be right back."

I take a quick breath to get rid of the tingly feeling where Braxton's arm touched mine. Selene watches him, her eyebrows drawn together, as he goes back to the bar. She hates it when he flirts with me like that—always has.

I brush my hair back from my forehead. I don't know if it's because Braxton was sitting so close to me, but I'm feeling warm and flushed. I glance over at Derek, but he's wrapped up in conversation with his old friend. I hate to admit it, but I'm glad he's not here. It feels good to be with just Braxton and Selene again. It's been too long.

Braxton comes back, and a minute later the bartender brings three tequila shots on a tray, along with a little plate of sliced limes and a salt shaker.

"Thank you, my good man," Braxton says. He passes out the shot glasses, and we all take a slice of lime and put a little salt on our hand, next to our thumb.

We hold up our shot glasses.

"To Kylie," he says.

We lift our glasses, then lick the salt and take the shot, following it with lime. It burns going down. Normally I like doing a few shots of tequila, but tonight even the first one doesn't sit well. I immediately feel a little sick.

I grab one of the waters on the table and take a sip. I'm probably just dehydrated.

"So…" I say, looking at Braxton. "Single again, I hear?"

He smiles again and the tingles are back. Why does he keep smiling at me like that? It's not fair. I can't think straight. "You didn't know?" he asks.

I shake my head. I can't quite talk yet.

He shrugs, completely nonchalant. "Yeah, wasn't working out." He meets my eyes. "But at least now I'm open to the right thing when it does come along."

"That's good," I say. I take another sip of water. "I wasn't going to say anything, but I'm relieved."

"Are you?" he asks. "Tell me."

"Oh, I don't know, I figure this must be good for your budget. How much were you spending on jewelry? Like, in a given week?"

He raises his eyebrows and smirks. "Thousands, at least. Imagine all the extra money I'll have now. I wonder what I should do with it?"

"Clearly spend it on me," I say. "I could do with a new car, and my apartment needs new furniture, so…"

"I can do something about that," he says. "When should we go shopping?"

"As soon as possible," I say.

"Sounds good," he says. "You need some new panties too? Because I'd be happy to take care of that for you."

"Braxton!" Selene says.

He grins and raises his eyebrows at her.

"You're the worst," Selene says with a laugh.

"You know what?" he says. "We need another shot. To celebrate my greatly enhanced budget."

I'm not so sure that's a good idea, but he gets up and goes back to the bar before I can protest.

"Are you okay?" Selene asks. "You look a little red."

I pull on my shirt to fan some air onto my boobs. "Is it warm in here?"

"I'm not warm, but Braxton forgot about personal space again. Maybe that's it."

I take another sip of water. "Yeah, could be."

Braxton returns and we all do another shot of tequila. I sit back while he chats with Selene. I go from feeling too warm to almost shivering with cold. I move a little closer to Braxton, letting my arm lean on his. He shifts his leg so it's touching mine. For half a second, I think maybe we shouldn't be sitting like this, but his body heat seeps into me, so I don't pull away.

Either the tequila is strong as fuck, or there's something wrong with me. My body feels like it's turning to water, and my face is burning. I lean my forearms on the table and almost put my head down.

This isn't good.

Selene's eyes are wide with alarm. "Oh my god, Kylie, what's wrong?"

"Ky?" Braxton says. His brow is furrowed and he puts a hand on my forehead. "She's hot as hell."

"Excuse me?" Derek says. He's standing at the end of the table, glaring at Braxton.

"Hey man, I think she needs to get home—"

"Yeah, fuck off, I've got this," Derek says.

I feel Braxton tense up next to me, but he doesn't say anything, just gets out of the booth.

I can barely stand up. My legs don't want to support my weight, and my head is swimming. It's like coming to after a drunken blackout, only I haven't lost time and I'm not drunk. I barely feel the two shots of tequila, and I had all of three sips of my beer. I put a hand on my forehead and lean against the table.

"Shit," I say.

Braxton stands up and grabs my arm to steady me. "Are you okay, Ky? What's wrong?"

"I'll take her home," Derek says. He puts an arm around me—roughly, like he's angry—and pulls me toward the door. I stumble forward, my vision fuzzy. I have to clutch onto him when we get outside, so I don't fall over.

He gets me to his car and I can't even fasten the seatbelt. My arms feel weak and my stomach is churning. Derek gets in without a word and starts the car. I lean my head back against the seat, and close my eyes. I can't keep them open. I don't know what's happening, but I'm caught between burning up and freezing cold, and it feels like my limbs won't work. All I want is to get home and crawl into bed.

What the fuck is happening to me?

14

BRAXTON

I wait as long as I can stand before making an excuse to Selene about needing to leave. She was concerned too, but seemed unreasonably certain that Derek would get Kylie home and she'd be fine.

I don't give a fuck what Derek will or won't do. I'm worried out of my mind for Ky. She deteriorated so fast. Her face lost all its color, and there were deep dark circles under her eyes.

I race over to her apartment and find a spot across the street. I don't see Derek's car out front, but he could have parked around the block. I hope he didn't make her walk too far. I wouldn't be surprised if he had to carry her inside. I run up to the door and knock. At this point, I know it looks weird for me to come over, and Derek's going to be pissed. But fuck it. I don't give two shits.

No one answers. I knock again. Maybe he took her to the hospital. Is she that sick?

I put my ear to the door, listening. I definitely hear something. In fact, I'm sure she's in there. I decide I don't care if Derek knows I have a key. I put it in, but the door isn't locked.

The smell of vomit hits me like a truck as soon as I walk in. It's sickly sweet and very fresh. It's all over the floor, trailing up the short hallway. My stomach turns at the sight.

I hear Ky heaving, then a splash of water. Shit. I run down the hall, careful not to step in the puke.

I find her on her knees in front of the toilet, leaning forward, her hands on her thighs. Her back moves up and down as she takes big breaths.

"Kylie," I say. There's more vomit on the floor. I grab a towel, I don't even give a fuck which one, and wipe it to the side so I can kneel next to her.

"Braxton?" she says, her voice weak.

"Yeah, baby girl. Where's Derek?"

"He dropped me off," she says.

What in the actual fuck? "He left you like this?"

"I threw up in his new car."

I'm so mad I almost can't see straight, but Ky sounds so miserable. She groans, clutching her stomach.

"Are you gonna throw up more?" I ask. I rub my hand across her back.

She nods. I pull her hair back—some of it's wet, but I ignore that—and keep it out of her way while her body convulses. I don't think there's anything left for her to throw up. She heaves and gags, but not much comes out. She's pretty empty.

She sits back on her heels, taking shuddering breaths. I keep her hair back in case she isn't done. She closes her eyes and seems to relax a little. I try to ignore the smell, not let it touch me.

"I think I'm done," she says, flushing the toilet. "For now, I guess."

"Can you stand?" I ask.

"Maybe."

I let go of her hair and take her hands, helping her to her feet. She's got puke all over—it's in her hair, soaking the front of her shirt, and on her skirt.

"You need a shower," I say, but I immediately know I'm not letting her take one alone. She looks so weak, I don't know if she can hold herself up.

"I'm freezing."

I glance around the bathroom, trying to think of how to make this work. She's filthy. I can't believe I'm about to do this. She's with Derek. He should be the one taking care of her, showering her off.

Oh well, fuck you, Derek. You left her here when she's sick, you douche.

I untie her halter top at the back of her neck and gently pull it over her head.

"What are you doing?" she asks.

"Let's get you cleaned up so you can lie down."

She doesn't protest as I take off her skirt, just stands there in a strapless bra and black panties, shivering. It's not cold in the bathroom, and her cheeks are flushed red, but she acts like she's outside in the middle of winter.

I turn on the shower. How am I going to manage this? I can't get her naked, can I? Can she stand up long enough to get clean? She's already swaying on her feet.

Fuck it. I pull off my shirt and strip down to my underwear. She hugs her arms around herself, still shivering, and I notice that her bra looks wet. The puke probably soaked through her shirt.

I decide I'll just keep her turned away from me, and keep my underwear on. Steam pours out from the shower stall, so I adjust the temperature. I put gentle hands on her shoulders, turn her around, and unhook her bra. She widens her arms, letting it fall to the floor. Then she sticks her thumbs in the waistband of her panties and pushes them down.

I help her take them off. Fuck, I've wanted to take the panties off this woman for so long, but not like this. Never like this. She's shaking, and her skin is burning hot to the touch.

I guide her into the shower and get in with her in case she falls. Her legs almost buckle, and I have to put my hands around her waist to hold her up. My heart pounds. I try to keep my eyes off her bare ass.

I look away and close my eyes while she turns to wet her hair. She doesn't say a word. When she turns around again, I use her shampoo to wash her hair. I don't linger, don't massage her scalp and turn it into a back rub that becomes fucking her from behind. It's what I want to do—desperately—but she's trembling and weak.

And Selene would murder me.

I take her body wash off the ledge and open it for her. The smell hits my nose, and I'm reeling. It's her. Kylie in a fucking bottle. It's small and green and says *lilac breeze*. But it's her. I know this scent. I've been smelling it for years. It never really leaves my nose, no matter how long we go without seeing each other. I hold it up to my face and breathe it in, the scent mixing with the wet shower air.

Now *my* legs almost buckle.

I put some in her hand so she can finish washing, then avert my eyes again while she rinses off. She needs my help getting out. I can tell she's about to drop. I wrap a towel around myself, then one around her, and lead her into the bedroom.

She crawls into bed naked, her hair still dripping. I help extricate her from the towel and quickly pull the sheets and comforter around her. I try so hard not to look at her, not to see her beautiful body. It isn't for me.

I go to the kitchen and get her a glass of water. I make sure she only takes a tiny sip and take it away before she drinks more. I wonder if she wants to swish with mouthwash, but I don't want to do anything that will trigger more vomiting.

Her eyes are closed, so I leave her long enough to toss my wet underwear in her dryer and put my other clothes back on. Jeans with no underwear is the worst, but I don't want to walk around her apartment naked. I'm careful as I zip, because *fuck*.

I clean up the vomit in the hall and the bathroom, throwing all the towels in the wash. I find a container of cleaning wipes with bleach under the sink and go around the whole place, wiping everything down—doorknobs, handles, drawer pulls, light switches. I figure I'm probably going to get whatever virus she has—the fever makes me pretty sure it isn't food poisoning—but I don't care. I'm bigger and stronger than she is. I'll deal with it if I have to.

By the time the place is clean, my underwear are dry, so I gratefully put them back on. I go in to check on Ky. Her eyes flutter open and I grab the water to give her another sip.

"Hey," she says. Her skin is ashen and her lips a weird color of waxy blue. The circles under her eyes are worse, and a sheen of sweat glistens on her forehead.

"Shh," I say. "Don't talk. Just rest."

"I feel like I'm gonna die." There's a tinge of fear in her voice that makes my heart ache. She looks so tiny and frail, all wrapped up in blankets, her face so pale.

"You aren't going to die," I say. "I promise I won't let that happen."

"I puked in his car."

"Fuck his car." I'm dangerously close to breaking the unspoken pact—but he dropped her off when she's this sick? It isn't right. Anger fills me again. I take a breath, but hold back from saying anything about it. I don't want to make her feel worse. "Do you want more water?"

"No," she says. "I'm so cold. I can't get warm."

I touch her forehead. She's scalding hot, but she's shivering beneath the covers. "You have a fever."

"This sucks." Her whimper is so sad. I sit on the edge of the bed and touch her face, letting my fingers caress her burning skin. I should stop. This is how I've always wanted to touch her. Soft and familiar. Intimate. She's not mine to touch, and she's sick. Even if she wasn't, I know she won't cheat on Derek. I don't want her to. I won't have her like that.

I'd rather not have her at all.

That thought hurts way too much. I'm torturing myself, moving my hand across her forehead and down her face, like I have right to touch her this way. Like she's not my best friend.

I realize her eyes are wet with tears, and I stop, pulling my hand away. I clear my throat. "I'll let you rest. I'll be on the couch. If you need anything, just call for me."

"Please don't leave me."

Her voice is so soft, I'm not sure I hear her. But her huge eyes look up at me, pleading.

"No," I say, touching her face again. "I won't leave you. Not ever."

"I'm so cold."

She's still shivering. I know how to get her warm, but I don't want to do it. It shouldn't be me.

But I've already done this much, and she needs someone.

She should need Derek, but she has me.

I slip off my jeans and shirt, and crawl into bed with her. She's already on her side, so I get behind her and pull her body toward me, letting our skin touch. I'm very glad I dried my underwear already, because her bare ass on my cock would be an absolute disaster. As it is, I angle my groin away from her so she won't feel my hard-on. But I touch her with every other inch of my body.

She's so hot, I quickly begin to sweat, but I ignore the discomfort. At first she's shivering hard, but it doesn't take long before my body heat seeps into her. She relaxes against me and her violent shivers become a few tremors. Then her back is moving in a slow rhythm, her arms and legs loose. I hold on to her, my hands around her belly, my face near her still-damp hair. I'm completely surrounded by her scent. It's in her hair, on her skin, in her sheets. I'm floating in a sea of it, an ocean of lilac breeze.

I start to get uncomfortable, and I'm way too hot, but I don't move. I won't move until she needs me to. I hold her for dear life, wishing desperately for her to get better, wishing even more desperately that this moment will never end. That I'll never have to go back to the reality of our life. The reality where we are just friends and we date other people. Where I fuck girls I don't care about and feel like shit about it later. Where she dates guys who are too stupid to see how fucking special she is.

Our timing has always been shit, but this is worse than usual. I'm completely intoxicated by her body next to mine, but I won't do anything about it. I can't. She isn't mine to have, and unless something changes, I have to find a way to live with things the way they are.

But right now, in this moment—even though she's passed out with a fever—she *is* mine.

15

KYLIE

I wake up four days after puking in Derek's car. I hardly remember anything since leaving the bar. Sickness stole over me so quickly, I knew I was in trouble. I've spent the last four days in a haze of fever. I don't remember much.

Except Braxton.

Every time my eyes fluttered open, he was there, as if he was doing nothing but waiting for me to wake up. He gave me water in little sips, and later something that tasted like watered-down Gatorade. He helped me go to the bathroom, his arms around me while I shuffled down the hall, almost too weak to stand. It didn't escape my notice that he cleaned up the puke from when I spewed all over trying to run to the toilet.

He slept next to me, in my bed. We didn't talk about it; he just did. I'm grateful as shit, especially because the first night, I woke up needing to hurl again. He was up in an instant, putting a glass bowl in front of me so I wouldn't get it on the bed. Then he cleaned me up and tucked me back in bed, holding me tight against him. I shivered, so cold, until his body heat warmed me, cutting through the shakes the fever gave me. I slept soundly. I was no longer afraid.

I realize the worst must be over when I wake up hungry. Brax isn't in bed, but I know he's still here. I can hear faint sounds coming from the kitchen, but it isn't that. I just know. I can feel his presence in my apartment. His magnetism.

My bed smells like him. It's such a strange thing, but it smells so good that I lean my head into the pillow he's been using and breathe it in.

This is wrong. Really wrong. He's been the absolute best friend in the entire world, taking care of me when I was sick. I should not be thinking these thoughts about him. Plus, I'm with Derek. I have a boyfriend, and it's kind of serious—serious enough that doing anything with Brax would absolutely be cheating.

And fuck, it's Braxton. Never mind how incredible it's been to have him here, sleeping beside me. How my body molds to his, fitting like we're two puzzle pieces. How deeply touched I am that he would do this for me—stay with me for days, wait on me hand and foot, clean up my fucking puke.

We've been friends for a long time, and we've always been there for each other when things are rough, but this is on another level.

I've been deliriously sick for days and I don't remember getting any phone calls or texts. That seems odd, especially because I'd think Derek would have called. My breath freezes in my chest. Did he call and talk to Brax? Shit, that isn't good.

My phone is on the nightstand, but it's turned off. I power it back on and look to see if I have any voicemails or missed calls. There's a voicemail from my dad that's two days old, and a few texts from Selene. But there's nothing from Derek.

Braxton appears in the doorway, leaning against the frame. "I knew you looked better this morning," he says.

I blink at him, still feeling disoriented. I'm having trouble remembering what's real and what was a fever dream.

The shower has to be a dream. There's no way he showered with me like that.

"Yeah," I say, sitting up in bed. I'm wearing a loose t-shirt with no bra, and plain cotton underwear. Maybe I should feel self-conscious about being half-naked, but I don't. I'm pretty sure Brax dressed me, and somehow that isn't weird. I glance down at my phone again. "Has my phone been off the whole time?"

"Yeah, sorry," he says. "I turned it off so it wouldn't disturb you. You weren't in any state to talk to people anyway."

"No," I say. Did Derek really not call? "Thanks."

"Are you hungry yet?"

"I think I'm starving, but it's hard to tell," I say. My stomach feels empty, but very raw. "I'm a little bit scared to eat anything."

"I'll get you some soup," he says. "We'll start off slow."

"Brax, you don't have to do that," I say.

He shrugs. "It's fine. I'm hungry anyway." He walks away before I can say anything else.

I check again to see if there's any way I'm not seeing Derek's calls. I puked in his car, and ran off to my apartment with my hand clamped to my mouth, still vomiting. It was pretty obvious I was sick. Would he really leave me here and not call to see if I'm okay? That seems unlikely.

Still, I wonder what's going on, so I bring up his number and hit send.

"Hi," he says.

"Hey," I say. "Are you busy?"

"Just prepping for the game tomorrow." He sounds irritated.

"Sorry, I don't mean to bother you. I just ... I haven't talked to you for a while. My phone was turned off, so I'm sorry if you tried to call."

"I didn't."

"You didn't try to call?" I ask.

"No."

"Derek, you saw how sick I was. You didn't wonder if I was okay?"

"You puked all over my brand new car," he says, "and it's not like you've called me to apologize."

My mouth drops open. I cannot believe what I'm hearing. "Are you serious? You've been waiting for four days for me to call you to say sorry I puked in your new fucking car?"

"Well, shit, it was gross," he says. "I had to spend three hundred dollars getting it detailed, and they couldn't fit me in until yesterday. I couldn't even get in the car, it smelled so bad."

"I've been so sick I couldn't get out of bed," I say, my voice rising. I don't want Braxton to hear us fight, but I'm so mad I can't help it. "I couldn't make it to the bathroom without help. And you're worried about your goddamn car?"

"I didn't know you were sick," he says.

"Because you didn't call to find out. Besides, wasn't it obvious?"

"Son of a bitch, Kylie, I thought you had too much to drink. You and that fucker Braxton were pounding shots like you were at a goddamn frat party."

"I had two shots, asshole," I say. "Two."

He's quiet for a second. "It seemed like it must have been more."

"No, it wasn't," I say. "And I'll pay you back for the stupid car detailing."

"No, no," he says. "Fuck, I'm sorry. I honestly had no idea. I thought Braxton got you drunk, and it pissed me off. I didn't know you were sick. Are you okay?"

"Yeah," I say. I'm not going to tell him it was Brax who took care of me. It will only piss him off, and I don't have the energy to fight with him right now.

I look up and see Braxton standing in the doorway. He has a tray with a steaming bowl of soup, a glass of ice water, and a little stack of saltine crackers. There's no way he had time to heat up soup while I've been on the phone. That means he made it for me before I woke up.

Holy shit.

"I'm glad you're okay, babe," Derek says.

I stare at Braxton. His stubble is thicker than usual and he's wearing the same clothes he had on at the bar the other night. He's literally been here this whole time, hasn't he?

Vaguely, I remember begging him not to leave me the first night I was sick. And he didn't. Brax stuck. I'm stunned —and extremely confused—because what I'm feeling is not a feeling I should have for Braxton.

"Kylie?" Derek says.

"Sorry, I'm still really tired. I'll talk to you later."

"Okay, bye babe," Derek says.

Braxton's eyes are on the floor as I hang up. I can tell he knows who I was talking to. When he looks up at me, I see something I've never seen on his face before. Pain.

I've seen him in physical pain. I was with him after his motorcycle accident. His leg was mangled. He kept it in pretty well, but I saw it in his eyes while I sat with him in his hospital room.

But this pain is different. It's deeper. More personal.

No, he can't be in pain over me. It has nothing to do with Derek, or sleeping next to me in my bed these last four days. He's only doing what a best friend does. That's why we're so great together. We take care of each other.

We *are* great together.

Fuck.

A new thought bursts through my mind, ravaging my brain with its truth. But it isn't new at all. It's a thought I've had for years. I just keep pushing it away, ignoring it. Looking at Braxton, standing in my doorway with a tray of soup he made for me, I can't make it stop. I can't get it out of my mind any more than I can ignore how it's felt to have him with me these last four days.

I'm completely, totally, madly in love with him.

16

KYLIE

There is absolutely no question in my mind that I have to end it with Derek. It isn't fair to either of us. I'm not even mad about the night I got sick. It was a dick move on his part, but it isn't a deal breaker.

Braxton is the deal breaker.

I'll simply tell Derek I don't see our relationship going anywhere, and I think we should go our separate ways. I don't know whether he'll even care very much. When we first started dating, he seemed totally into me, but lately I'm left wondering if he'd notice if we didn't see each other for a long time.

Regardless of my recent revelation, Derek and I don't have a future, and I know it.

I have no clue what I'm going to do about Braxton. I'm a mess. Telling him the truth is completely out of the question. There is no way I can let this slip. We've been friends for too long, and this threatens every fiber of that friendship. Despite the way he looks at me sometimes, I can't imagine he feels the same way. He's just a shameless flirt. He's not serious about any woman, so I can't expect that he'd magically be serious about me. And the last thing I need is to become another notch on Braxton's bedpost.

I try for almost a week to see Derek in person, but he always has a reason he can't. I don't want to do this over the phone, but I decide I can't take the waiting anymore, and call him.

"Hey, babe," he says. He sounds distracted.

"Derek, do you have a minute to talk?" I say. "Is this a good time?"

"Yeah, sure," he says.

"Listen, I didn't want to do this over the phone, but I keep trying to get together, and you're always too busy," I say.

"Okay."

I take a deep breath. "I don't think we should see each other anymore." There, I said it.

Derek is quiet for a long moment. "Are you serious?"

"Yes," I say. "I'm so sorry, Derek. You're a great guy, but ... we're not great together. We're just okay. I want more than okay."

I hear him take a breath. "Yeah, I kind of knew this was coming. It sucks, Kylie. You're a great girl."

"Thanks," I say. "I just ... I can't pretend, you know? I realized this isn't going anywhere. We both deserve better than that."

"I suppose we do," he says.

Wow. This is, like, the easiest breakup I've ever had. We don't even have stuff at each other's places to worry about. "You okay?"

"Sure," he says. "I'll be fine. Take care, Kylie. It's been real."

"Yeah, you too."

I hang up and sink down into the couch. I'm so grateful

that's over. It's a ding to my pride that he didn't try to change my mind, but I suppose that confirms I did the right thing.

Now what?

I need to tell Selene. Maybe she'll be inspired to dump Matthew. She never has anything nice to say about their relationship anymore.

But it's not Selene who floods my mind. It's Braxton.

I wouldn't normally get hold of him just to tell him I broke up with someone—not unless I was heartbroken and wanted to cry on his shoulder, which has happened more times than I'd like to admit.

I'm certainly not heartbroken now. But Derek was his client. I should give him a heads up. Just because of the impact to his business. That's all.

I could text him, but I find myself dialing his number.

"Hey, baby girl," he says.

My heart wants to leap out of my chest at the sound of his voice.

"Hi, Brax," I say. *Go on. Just say it.* "If you're not busy, do you want to grab dinner?"

Wait, why did I say that? I don't need to do this in person.

"Love to," he says. "Tonight?"

"Sure," I say. Okay, this is fine. "Meet me at Brody's in an hour?"

"I'll be there," he says.

I SIT in a booth at the back of the restaurant. I'm glad they gave me this spot. I feel protected back here, without many customers nearby. I'm so jumpy, my heart feels like it's going to beat out of my chest.

Braxton comes in, sunglasses on his face. Fuck, he's beautiful. His muscles strain against his black shirt; his jeans drape perfectly down his strong legs. I can't see his ass but I know how amazing it is, especially in those jeans. He pulls his sunglasses off and grins at me across the restaurant.

My tummy flutters like I'm a little girl with a crush. I smile and take a quick sip of water. Why am I so nervous? All I want to do is tell him I broke up with Derek. That shouldn't be a big deal. He and I have been through more than our share of relationships over the years. Why does this feel like such momentous news? Like everything is going to change when I tell him?

He slides into the booth, and a waitress appears. She looks admiringly at him, more or less ignoring me. It pisses me off. I want to push her away from the table and tell her to stop fucking looking at him.

I take a deep breath. Wow, I'm really tense. I need to calm down, or I'm going to do something stupid. Very stupid.

Braxton orders a beer, and the waitress asks if I want a drink. I stick with water. I don't want to drink tonight. I need all of my inhibitions in full force. I need a fucking wall of inhibitions to protect me. I cannot let him see what I'm feeling.

"You look great," he says.

"Thanks," I say. I haven't seen him since the day he made me soup. Since the day I realized... *No, don't think about that, Kylie.* "It's nice to be in the land of the living again."

"No shit."

The waitress brings his beer. He winks at her and my back tightens.

This. *This* is why I have to keep these horribly traitorous feelings to myself. Braxton is a player to the zillionth degree. He'll probably get that waitress's phone number and fuck her before the week is out.

I am not equipped to deal with him.

"So, what's up?" he asks. "Other than you need to fucking eat something. You look like you lost ten pounds."

I did lose weight when I was sick, and it isn't the good way to lose it. My face looks pretty gaunt. "I know, right?" I force a casual tone that I do not feel. "I think I'll have a burger and fries. Maybe we should get an appetizer. Wanna share something? Onion rings sound really good."

I'm talking too fast, and Brax looks at me like he can tell there's something going on. "You okay?"

"Sure, it's just been too long since I got out of the house."

He nods, but I see in his face that he doesn't believe me. The waitress returns and he orders three appetizers. "You need to put some meat back on," he says after she leaves.

"I broke up with Derek." I blurt out the words before I can think.

Braxton's face goes still, his eyes burning with intensity. He stares at me and his chest moves faster, his breath quickening. "What?"

Oh, shit. He's pissed. I should have talked to him first. Derek was his client.

"I'm sorry, I know he was your client," I say. "I hope this doesn't mess anything up with your business."

His eyebrows draw together. "Business? No. No, I don't care."

I swallow hard. Why is he looking at me like that? I expect him to laugh, and start cracking jokes about what a douche Derek is. That's what he always does when I break up with someone. "Okay, well, that's good," I say. "Because I ended it with him a few hours ago."

He leans forward, resting his forearms on the table. "Are you fucking serious?"

He is not making me any less jittery. I feel like I'm going to jump out of my own skin. Does he think I made a mistake? "Yes."

His eyes don't move. They hold onto mine, locking them in place. I have no idea what is happening around me. There is nothing but Braxton's dark eyes.

"Are you going to say something?" I ask.

He doesn't. I don't know what I want him to do, but he does nothing. Just stares at me.

"Why?" he asks, finally.

I'm so surprised by the question, I'm not sure what to say. I can't very well tell him the truth. "I guess it wasn't working. He's not a bad guy, and I care about him. But that's not enough."

"It's not enough," he says. Suddenly he's next to me, on my side of the booth. I scoot away, but his legs touch mine and his body is so close. He's so much larger than me. He takes up all the space, sucks away all the air. I can barely breathe.

"I don't know if I should do this," he says in a low voice. His face is so close. "But I can't let this go. Not again." He looks away. That pain is in his eyes again, the one I saw at my place when I was sick.

He turns back to me, his face hard with resolve. He leans in, moving closer, his eyes on my mouth.

Oh my god, he's going to kiss me.

I want him to, desperately. But if he kisses me, everything changes. We've never kissed. Never fooled around. As many times as we've been drunk off our asses together, nothing physical has ever transpired between us, innocent or otherwise. It's a line we both know cannot be crossed.

Like our unspoken pact about talking about our relationships. It's what makes our friendship work. What makes us last.

His nose brushes mine and I tilt my face, giving him a clear path. He puts a hand on my arm and I tremble at his touch. His hand is hot on my skin. My heart races.

At first his lips barely brush against mine. He's holding back, and I'm shocked to realize he's trembling as much as I am. Electricity lights me up, shooting through my lips, straight to my chest. I suck in a little breath.

His lips press harder, and my eyes drift closed. I'm melting, my body turning to water, running down the seat and making a puddle on the floor. His scent floods through me, masculine, warm, familiar.

The kiss grows as we both relax into it. Vaguely, I'm aware we're in a restaurant and perhaps food has just been set on the table. I don't care.

He kisses me slowly. It's not at all how I thought he would kiss. Braxton is brash and aggressive, but this kiss is sweet. Almost reverent. I open my lips and his tongue darts in, just a taste. Every move he makes is careful, tender.

Our lips part, and we hesitate there, breath on each other's faces. My eyes are closed. I can't bear to open them. I'm afraid that if I do I'll wake up and realize this has all been another fever dream.

I'm dazed, but I open my eyes. Braxton is there, his eyes fierce. He leans his face beside mine, his mouth right at my ear, and makes a low noise in his throat. "Oh god, Kylie. I've wanted to do that for so long."

I'm utterly frozen. I can't remember how to speak.

"If you say yes," he growls in my ear, "we are going to walk out of here right now, go back to my place, and I'm going to fuck you like no one has ever fucked you before, or ever will again."

My voice is nothing but a whisper. "What?"

"But you have to tell me yes," he says. "You have to say you want this."

"Yes." I'm incapable of any other answer.

He pulls out his wallet and tosses a hundred-dollar bill on the table in the midst of our appetizers. Then he grabs my hand and pulls me out of the booth.

There are eyes on us as we leave, but we're out the door so quickly they don't matter. He only lives a few blocks away, so we walk up the street toward his condo. He holds my hand, twining his fingers through mine like we're a normal couple out for an evening walk.

I'm terrified. What just happened? I was prepared for Braxton to laugh and make jokes, give me a good-natured hug to help me feel better. Maybe offer to get shit-faced with me. I was prepared to hold my feelings in, keep them on lockdown, make sure he couldn't see what was happening inside me.

Instead, I'm quickly realizing he feels something, too. Something besides a long friendship.

It's not long before we're at his door. He takes out his keys and fits one into the lock. I'm bursting with adrenaline, my fight or flight response going crazy.

He pulls me inside, his hand still enveloping mine, and closes the door behind us. He pushes me back against the door, standing over me. He's a big man, but he's never made me feel small until this moment—probably because he's never been this close for so long.

His eyes are all over my face, like he's trying to memorize me. He holds himself up with one hand, while his other slips around my waist. It fits there perfectly, like he was always meant to hold me.

"Are you sure about this?" I ask.

"I've never been more sure of anything."

I want to ask about Selene. What is she going to think? She's going to be pissed—we both know that—but I don't want him to stop looking at me this way.

"What if this is a mistake?" I ask.

"It isn't," he says, his voice forceful. Vehement. "It can't be a mistake."

I don't want to lose him. When this ends, when we crash and burn—because this is Braxton and I know how this ends—I don't want us to be over forever. How would I live without him?

But I'm too far gone to let that stop me now.

He glides his hand up my waist, brushing the side of my breast, up to my neck. He wraps his hand around the back of my head, his grip firm.

"I want you, Kylie," he says. "I've wanted you for longer than you can imagine."

Words completely fail me. I stare at him; his face is so close, his eyes boring through to my soul.

He takes my mouth with his—fucking takes it, like it belongs to him and always has. This is the kiss I expect from Braxton. Hard. Determined. Possessive. His hand holds my head in a steel grip, his lips firm. His tongue caresses mine, luxurious but forceful. I couldn't keep my eyes open if I tried, and my mind goes blank. He's completely overwhelming, kissing me in a way I've never been kissed in my entire life. I've never felt so open, so vulnerable. So needed.

I run my hands up his chest and grab his shirt, like I need to cling to him to keep from drowning. Our kiss deepens, sweeping me away with its power.

He pulls away and I try to follow. I don't want him to stop.

"I'm going to show you, baby girl," he says, running his thumb over my bottom lip.

"Show me what?" Apparently I can still form words.

"Everything," he says. "Everything I've ever felt for you. I'm going to love every inch of you tonight."

He kisses me again, running his fingers through my hair. Fuck, he's good at this. I'm completely in his control. He could do anything with me right now.

He leaves my mouth and kisses a trail down my neck. I tip my head back, leaning against the door. His body presses against mine and—

Oh shit, is that—

"Do you see what you do to me?" he says into my ear.

His cock is rock solid, pushing against my hip, and it feels … huge. Like, *holy shit is this for real?* huge.

"What do you think, baby?" he asks. "Do you want me to fuck you against the door? Or should I take you to my bed for our first time?"

My eyes roll back into my head. "I want you to fuck me everywhere."

He groans into my neck. His hands slide to my ass, and he hoists me up. I wrap my legs around his waist; he carries me to his bedroom, holding me like I weigh nothing.

He lays me down on his bed. I'm on fire with anticipation, my pussy hot, my body tingling. He pulls off his shirt and tosses it to the side, then slides off his pants. His cock bulges in his boxer briefs, almost sticking out the top. I've seen him shirtless a million times, but this time I don't have to pretend I don't notice. He's fucking perfect. Broad chest, rippling abs and holy shit, the *V*. It cuts down between his hips, like a muscular arrow pointing to his cock. He might as well have *Kylie, You Want This* written across his abs.

He raises an eyebrow at me, one corner of his mouth turning up in a grin.

"You are so sexy when you look at me like that," I say.

"Baby, I'll do anything to keep you talking to me that way," he says. He pushes his underwear down and kicks them off, revealing his magnificent cock, then smirks at me again.

"Like what you see?"

"Holy shit, Braxton," I say. "Is this really happening?"

"It's definitely happening," he says. "And it's going to keep happening."

He unbuttons my jeans and slides them off. My heart races. Is Braxton really undressing me? I sit up a little so he can pull my shirt over my head.

"This time," he says, "I don't have to look away. Turn over." He grabs my hips and flips me to my stomach. He unfastens my bra and I let the straps fall off my arms. Then he pushes his hands beneath my panties, sliding them down my legs.

I turn to look at him over my shoulder. "This time?"

"When you were sick, I had you naked in the shower. God, I wanted to touch you then. But holy fuck, look at that ass." He kneads his hands into my flesh.

"That really happened?" I ask. "I thought it was a fever dream."

"No, it was real," he says. "Too fucking real. But this—Kylie, this is worth the wait."

He grabs my legs and pulls me down so I'm tipped over the edge of the bed, my feet on the floor. He presses up against me and leans down so his body touches the entire length of mine. His skin on mine is sublime. I shudder at the feel of his heat, his skin, his cock pushing against my ass. He slips a hand beneath my belly and lifts my upper body. I tip upward, his chest against my back, and hold myself up with my arms. His hand trails down. He kisses across my shoulder, to my neck. His hand reaches between my legs and I gasp. He finds my clit instantly, like he already knows exactly where to touch me. Pleasure jolts through me, taking the breath from my lungs.

"Oh god, Braxton."

"Baby, I love hearing you say my name."

His finger flicks over my clit and my pussy heats up—fast. He massages gently, and my legs start to shake. It feels so good I can barely stand it. "How are you doing that?"

He nips the side of my neck with his teeth and I shudder. "I'm just getting you warmed up."

I lean my head back against his shoulder. One hand holds me around my waist while the other does some kind of crazy fucking magic on my clit. I have no idea what he's doing, but it feels unbelievable.

My breath comes faster and I rock my hips with the rhythm of his fingers. His cock digs into me from behind.

"Fuck, Braxton, you're going to make me come."

"Should I?" he says into my ear, his voice low and guttural. "Right here? Like this?"

I'm swirling, losing control. "Yes. Oh god, Braxton, make me come."

He groans and bites my shoulder. It pinches, but that only makes me hotter. I arch my back into him, pressing against his cock.

His fingers stop. I'm right on the edge, so close to orgasm it would take nothing more than another brush against my clit to send me over.

"Not yet," he says. "I want you to come on my cock."

He leans over and grabs a box of condoms from his nightstand. I don't really want to think about all the women he's been with, let alone bring it up with him right now—but fuck, I want him in me bare.

"Brax, have you been tested?" I ask. "Recently?"

He stops. "Yes. I always cover it, but yeah, I know I'm clean."

I meet his eyes. "Me too. I get the shot, so if you want..."

"Are you serious?" he says. His eyes move up and down my body and he quirks another smile.

I'm throbbing so hard I can barely think, but I know I'm sure about this. I want all of him. I turn over and crawl backwards onto the bed. "I don't want anything between us. Nothing."

He drops the condoms to the floor.

I scoot a little so he has room. He gets on top of me and settles between my legs, his cock just outside my opening. I want him inside me so bad I'm ready to beg for it, but his face is so serious.

He pauses, his nose brushing mine. "Are you ready for me?" he asks, his voice low.

"Yes."

"This is where it begins, Ky," he says. "This night."

"I know."

He slides in, slowly, carefully. His eyes roll back, closing, and he lets out a throaty moan.

Holy shit. The size of his cock was not an optical illusion. I'm so wet, he glides right in, but he stretches me open.

"More," I say. I grab his ass, trying to push him in deeper.

"Are you sure?"

"Yes, I want it all."

He plunges in further and, just when I think he's in to

the hilt, there's more. He buries himself inside me. I can feel the crown bottoming out, his girth filling me. He holds there, as if we're locked in place, our bodies melding together.

"Holy shit, Kylie, you feel so fucking good," he says.

I hold him against me, my arms around his back. He's deep inside me, but I want him closer. Deeper. Harder. I want him to take me and own me and never, ever let me go.

He pulls out and pushes in again, groaning into my neck.

"Fuck, Kylie, I want to take my time with you, but I don't think I can hold back."

"Don't hold back, Braxton," I say. "Fuck me hard. I want to still feel you in the morning."

Instantly, his weight on me eases, and he's fucking me hard. So hard. The world is gone, it's nothing, there's only me and Braxton and his cock moving so hard and so fast. It's everything. It's bliss. Every thrust is pure ecstasy. He pauses when I'm right on the edge, holding me there, making me ache for release.

"Oh fuck, Braxton."

"That's it, baby." He starts thrusting again. "Say my name."

"Braxton."

"Tell me what you want."

"Make me come, Braxton," I say, practically whimpering. "I want to come all over you."

"Oh, god, Ky, you're the sexiest fucking woman on this planet. I don't want this to end."

His cock pulses. I can feel how close he is to bursting.

"Don't stop that," I say. He hits my clit, perfectly, every time. I don't know how he does it. My muscles contract, my pussy clenching around him.

"Fuck, yes," he growls. "Fuck, fuck, yes."

He pounds hard, his body stiffening, his cock throbbing inside me, and suddenly I'm falling. Tumbling through the stars, out of control. I'm calling his name, riding the wave of his orgasm as he pours himself into me. My muscles tense and contract, over and over, until I forget to breathe.

I come down off the high, my breath coming fast. Braxton's body glistens in the dull light coming in through the window. He picks himself up, his cock still inside me. I keep my hands on his lower back, holding him in place. I want to stay connected.

He kisses my forehead, my cheeks, my chin, my jaw. His lips find mine and linger there, kissing me slowly, softly. I put my arms around his neck and drown in his kiss. I don't ever want to come up for air.

Eventually, he slides out and rolls onto his side. I miss him already; the inches between us are too much. He grabs me around the waist and pulls me into him. I tuck myself into his body, lying on my side with his arm draped over me. His feet tangle with mine. He cups my breast with one hand and rests his face next to my head.

We lie together, silent. We don't need to speak. My thighs are wet with his come; his sweat mingles with mine. His scent is all over me. He leans in and kisses my ear, my neck, my shoulder.

Nothing will ever be the same.

I want to cry with happiness—and fear. This is Braxton. My Braxton. I feel like I might burst. He holds me tight, like he's as afraid as I am that we'll wake up in the morning and realize none of it was real.

I want it to be real.

I close my eyes against the sting of tears. He holds my

fragile heart in the palm of his hand. His big, strong hand, that could crush it with no effort at all.

"Braxton?" I whisper.

He hugs me tighter, his muscles flexing around me. "Yes, baby?"

"Please don't break me."

"No," he says, his low voice fierce. "I promise. Not ever."

I close my eyes, hoping desperately it's a promise he can keep.

17

BRAXTON

I wake up with Kylie in my arms. My chest feels like it's going to burst, and it's all I can do to keep from crushing her against me.

I'm still a little giddy, basking in last night's glow. I probably look like a big idiot, but I can't stop smiling. She breathes evenly, her back moving against my chest. I want to let her sleep, but now that I'm awake I can't stop kissing her. My cock swells against her ass, and I kiss her ear, her neck, her shoulder.

Fuck, she's so good.

She's not just good. She's everything.

Our first time was too fast, but holy shit, she felt incredible. Better than any woman I've ever been with, and there's a long list of them. Every last one pales in comparison to Kylie. The taste of her skin on my tongue, the feel of her pussy wrapped around my cock. It was too much. I was coming in her long before I meant to, but she came hard all over me, so I didn't feel too bad about it. I fucked her two more times before we both fell asleep, exhausted, and those times I lasted longer.

Much longer.

I fill my nose with her scent, swim in lilac breeze. This time it isn't torture, it's heaven. There's nothing between us. Her bare skin is against mine. I've been inside her. I've filled every inch of her. Kissed her. Touched her. Held her.

And I don't have to stop.

She shifts her hips a little and makes a noise in her throat as she wakes up. She turns to look at me over her shoulder.

"Hey."

"Hi, baby girl," I say. I kiss her nose. "Did you sleep well?"

"How could I not?" she asks. "You wore me out last night."

"I'm going to wear you out every night."

She laughs. "Maybe let's take this one day at a time, okay?"

"Whatever you need, baby," I say. I kiss her shoulder again. "I'll make sure you want me every day." We lie in silence for a few minutes and I get a little nervous. Is she okay? Do we need to talk about this? "Ky?" I ask.

"Yeah?"

"Are you okay?"

She rolls onto her back and I prop my head up so I can look at her face. The sheet drapes across her belly, her gorgeous tits right there for me to see. I take her lack of modesty as a good sign. But her forehead is tight, a little groove forming between her eyebrows.

"I think so," she says.

"You're not sure?" I ask.

"I just..." She pauses, her eyes on the ceiling. "I didn't expect this to happen. I'm not sure *how* it happened. I mean, it's you. It's us."

"Are you glad?" I ask. *Please say yes.*

"Yes." She smiles, and I breathe out a sigh of relief. "Yes, I'm glad. But ... I didn't know you wanted me like this."

I raise my eyebrows. "Are you serious?"

"I had no idea," she says. "No, I guess that isn't true. I wondered. Sometimes the way you looked at me, or the things you said, made me think you might. But I figured you were just messing around, you know? I didn't think you meant it."

I touch her face, basking in the feel of her skin on my hand. "I meant it every single time."

"That's not possible," she says.

"Why not?"

"You've been flirting with me since we were teenagers."

"I've wanted you since we were teenagers," I say.

Her lips part. I can't wait to see those lips on my cock. The thought of it makes my dick stir.

"You have not," she says.

"I have, I swear." I lean down to kiss her, soft and sweet. She even tastes good first thing in the morning. "It's always been you, Kylie."

She stares at me again. "Why didn't you ever tell me?"

I look away. It's a good question. "I almost did, probably a thousand times. There was always something in the way. You were dating someone, or I was. And when we were both single, I don't know ... I didn't want to screw it up. We had this boundary we couldn't cross, and no matter how much I wanted to, I was afraid to risk it."

"What made you risk it last night?"

"After I broke up with Aubrey, I decided I was going to be ready for you the next time. I didn't care how long it took. If things ended with Derek, I would be there. I wasn't going to let another chance slip by. Because if I did, the next guy might be the one who took you from me forever. I couldn't let that happen."

She turns into me, and I wrap her in my arms. I kiss the top of her head. I can't wait to be inside her again, but more than anything, I'm just amazed that she's here, lying in bed with me.

"Kylie?" I ask. "Are you sure you're okay?"

She nods against my chest. "I'm more than okay."

I smile and hold her tight. She's soft and warm and delicious.

"So, what happens now?" she asks.

I nudge her onto her back and lean down to kiss her neck. I move down to her breasts and run my tongue across her nipple. I didn't get enough of these last night.

"Right now," I say, and lick her again. "We stay in bed. I'll make you breakfast later if you're hungry. But I want to savor you. I've been dreaming about this for years. I'm not finished yet."

She shivers as I graze my teeth on the hard nub of her nipple. "But, Brax," she says.

Her voice is too serious. I don't like it. It sounds like worries. "Yeah?"

"What are we going to tell Selene?"

I knew she was going to bring that up. I suppose it was inevitable, but I was hoping to fuck her again before we had to deal with that particular problem.

I shift back to my side and rest my head in my hand. I don't want to stop touching her tits—they're too fucking amazing to leave alone while they're uncovered like this—so I trace them with my finger.

"It's going to be a little difficult," I say. I might be understating that, but I don't want to alarm Kylie, and the truth is I don't know what Selene is going to think. "It will take her some time to get used to it."

"What if she's mad?"

I shrug. Mad doesn't bother me. Selene gets mad at me all the time. "She'll get over it."

"You say that like it doesn't matter," she says. "What if she's hurt?"

That word makes my throat constrict. I can't hurt my sister.

"The three of us have been friends for so long," Kylie continues. "And that's all we've ever been. If you and I are suddenly something else, Selene might not know how to process that. I've always felt like she didn't want me to like you that way, you know? Ever since we were kids. Every time I said something about you—how you looked or whatever—she was quick to shoot it down."

She's right, my sister is going to be tricky to handle. "Maybe we don't tell her right away."

"You want to lie to her?"

"Not exactly," I say. "But we can ease into this and talk to her when we're ready."

"So, we see where this goes first?" she asks.

I know exactly where I want this to go, and I hoped Kylie would be more certain than she sounds. But for now, I'll take what I can get. "Sure. We see where it goes. We'll know when it's time to tell her."

"Okay," she says. "What about today, then?"

"Today," I say, running my fingers down the line from her breasts to her belly button. "Today you can have whatever you want. Hard. Soft. Fast. Slow." I flick my fingers across her skin, like I'm ticking off her choices. "Mouth. Tongue. Cock. Forward, backward, sideways, upside-down. Anything. I still have so much to show you."

She laughs. "You're insatiable."

"I am when it's you," I say. "I've been a dying man in the desert, walking on the edge of a river, but the water was always out of reach. I've only just managed to jump in. I'm still thirsty."

"That's very *Greek tragedy* of you." She caresses my chest and runs her hand down my abs. "But I suppose it's appropriate when you look like a Greek god."

Her hand on my skin feels so good. "Mm, baby, keep doing that. It's helping."

"Speaking of water, maybe I should shower."

I grin at her. "I like you dirty."

"How dirty do you like me?"

I keep getting harder, passing the point where I can ignore it. I need her again. Now. "As dirty as I can get you," I say. I flip the sheet off her and she shivers, bending her knees to tuck her legs up closer. "Cold?"

"A little."

"I can help with that."

I nudge her legs open and slide my hand up the inside of her thigh. She's so fucking perfect—every curve, every mark, every angle. I lick my lips, and brush my fingers across the soft skin between her legs. She shivers again.

I grab a pillow and help her tuck it beneath her hips. She looks at me with her eyebrows drawn in.

"Trust me," I say.

I move so I'm in front of her and nibble my way up her inner thigh. She's breathing hard before I get anywhere near her pussy. The stubble on my jaw must be scratchy, but she seems to like it. I find a tiny freckle right at the crease of her leg and run my tongue across it.

"I owe you an apology," I say, and kiss her inner thigh again.

"For what?" she asks. I love how high-pitched and breathy she sounds.

"I was too preoccupied with my dick last night," I say. I kiss just outside her opening and lick my lips. Oh fuck, she tastes good.

"Your dick is magnificent," she says. "You should be apologizing for keeping it from me all these years."

"Baby, your pussy is fucking unreal." I slide my tongue between her wet folds. "I wish I could have had this a long time ago."

"Maybe we weren't ready then," she says.

I look up and meet her eyes. "Are you ready now?"

She tips her legs open for me. "Fuck, yes."

I dive in, eager to taste her, to feel her hot, wet skin against my tongue. Her hips are tipped up just right, and I swirl my tongue around her clit.

She grabs the sheets, shuddering. "Oh god, Braxton."

I want to keep hearing her say my name. I want to be the only name she ever calls out for the rest of her life.

I flick her clit with my tongue, testing her, seeing what she likes. I have so much to learn, so much to discover. I want to know it all. I give her more pressure and she rocks her hips up and down. I move with her, increasing my pace. My tongue slips back and forth across her clit, teasing her center.

I slide the pillow out so her hips turn up a little more and push my tongue inside her.

"Holy shit," she breathes.

I fuck her with my tongue, in and out, sliding it along the top of her opening where she's sensitive. Her heat builds and she bucks her hips against me. I hold her hips, moving them up and down, my tongue relentless. I want to see how fast I can make her come, so I speed up. She arches her back, her fingers tearing at the sheets. She pants with every thrust of my tongue.

"Oh fuck, Braxton, yes," she says in between breaths. "Yes, yes, yes."

I feel her pussy throb and clench as she comes. I don't let up. I want to stretch it out, drive her crazy, keep her coming forever. She calls my name, and I'm so hard that I'm tempted to reach down and jerk off while she finishes—but if I do it right, I think I can get her to come again immediately.

Her hips slow down and I feel her spasms subsiding. Before it's over, I push into her clit with the flat of my tongue and start again, flicking it fast.

"What the fuck?" she breathes.

Her thighs clench, and I push them open. Her body writhes; she calls out, loud and incoherent. She's completely losing control. I feel her on the brink of another orgasm, but I can't stand it anymore. I get up on my knees and rip the pillow out from under her, grab her hips and turn her over, pulling her ass up so she's on her knees, and press my hand into the middle of her back, pushing her upper body down.

I hold her hips and thrust into her pussy. I lean my head back and revel in the feel of her. She takes my whole length, as deep as I can go, sheathing me in her perfection. I hold there, tight against her, my cock buried inside her. I'm high as fuck, drunk on her taste, her smell, the feel of her pussy clamping around me.

"Holy shit, Braxton, fuck me now," she says.

I love that I can do this to her, make her hot and desperate. I thrust in and out, pounding her as hard as I dare. I don't want her hurt her, but she moans and leans into me, grinding her hips against me each time I plunge in.

The pressure builds, heat rushing to my groin, my balls tightening as they ready to empty into her. It's been years since I've been inside a woman without a condom, and there's absolutely nothing like the feel of my cock sliding against her bare flesh. I watch her ass, beautiful and round, lifted for me. God, she's amazing. I can't get enough of her.

Her pussy tightens around me. She's going to come again. I shouldn't have made her wait this long. I'll send her over the edge now, and wait to loose my cock in her. Then I can give her a third, and we can come together.

I lean down to sweep my arm under her ribcage and pull her upper body against me. My chest presses into her back and I reach around to finger her clit. I thrust my cock in, deep, and flick her clit twice. She throws her head back against my shoulder, coming hard. Her pussy clenching around my dick almost unmakes me, but I hold back, rubbing her clit until she finishes.

I'm so close, but I carefully pull out and turn her on her back. I give her a second to catch her breath, my cock so hard I feel like I could explode right here and come all over her tits.

She raises her arms over her head and her tits move up and down as she breathes. Her legs are bent and tipped open, as if she doesn't have the energy to move them anymore.

"Oh my god, Braxton," she says, wiping her hand across her forehead. "I don't even ... holy shit."

"One more, baby," I say.

I get on my knees and drag her closer. I push my cock in and thrust a few times. At first I think she might be too tired to come again. Her eyes are half closed, her lips partially open, and she's still breathing hard. But I swipe my thumb across her clit while I move in and out, and I feel her body come back to life.

"You have got to be fucking kidding me," she says.

Her eyes meet mine and the fire returns. I massage her clit as I thrust in and out, never looking away from her. I want her to know; I want her to feel everything I've felt for more years than I care to count. There aren't enough words for me to tell her, but I can show her with my body—my hands, my mouth, my cock. I want to show her what she is to me. What she's always been to me.

I want her to know this is real.

"Tell me when, baby girl," I say. I'm right on the brink, my dick aching with the need to unload in her.

"I can't believe…" She pants, bucking her hips. "Oh god, yes. Now, baby. Do it now."

I unleash and my cock throbs, pulsing over and over. I spill out into her, coating her, claiming her. My body stiffens and there's nothing but this wave of agonizing bliss washing over me. I think it's over, but there's more, pulse after pulse of ecstasy.

I slow down as the throbbing subsides. We're both slick with sweat, breathing hard. Kylie stares at me, those beautiful blue-gray eyes taking me in, her inky dark hair spilling across the bed. Her cheeks are flushed, her lips pink and full. I lean down and brush her hair back from her face. I kiss her mouth, tasting her sweet lips. I kiss her forehead, her cheeks, the base of her jaw just below her ear.

"Kylie," I whisper. There's nothing more. I just want to say her name.

"Braxton."

I lean my forehead gently against hers and smile. My heart wants to burst right out of my chest. She's the only thing I ever really wanted for myself, and the one thing I didn't think I would ever have.

But now, finally, she is mine.

18

BRAXTON

A couple weeks go by, and Kylie is my world. She goes home long enough to grab some clothes and brings them back to my condo. As far as I'm concerned, we should get rid of her apartment now, but I don't say it. She's still a little hesitant, although every night I easily convince her to stay over. I don't want to be without her.

I go to my gym and train my clients, but rush home when I'm done, hoping she'll be back from work. Just seeing her car parked on the street outside makes me smile.

I wake up every morning with her scent on my sheets, her hair draped across my pillow, and I can't believe how fucking lucky I am.

On Friday, I take her out to dinner. I purposefully avoid bringing her to any of our usual places. I don't want to risk running into Selene unexpectedly. Kylie and I haven't talked about Selene again, but I don't have to hear her say it to know she's nervous about my sister. I want to assure her I'll handle it, but the truth is, I'm not sure how.

Selene has always given me the death stare when I show interest in Kylie. Any time I let my guard down and looked at Ky with any sort of honesty—whether it was intentional or not—Selene would tense up and narrow her eyes at me. Sometimes I can almost feel what Selene is feeling—it's a twin thing, I guess—and when I would flirt with Kylie, I could feel Selene's anger. I know she's going to be mad at me for being with Ky. I just need some time to think about what to say to make her understand, and reassure her this doesn't mean she's losing Kylie to me. It will be different, but that doesn't have to be bad.

I have one client in the morning on Saturday, and when I finish, I have a text from Selene. A wave of nerves twists my gut. Shit. Her garbage disposal is broken and she wants me to come take a look at it. For a second, I think about telling her to get her dickhead boyfriend to come deal with it. But I always take care of Selene's house when something breaks. I always take care of my sister. It's what I do.

Kylie's having lunch with her dad, and I don't want to tell Selene anything without Ky being there. I figure Selene has no reason to suspect something, so I put the worry out of my mind. I'll go to her house and fix her disposal. Kylie and I can talk tonight about what to say to her. I don't know if Kylie is hesitant to tell her because she's afraid of Selene's reaction, or because she doesn't know if we're going to last. I hate the thought that she feels that way, but I can't really blame her. My history doesn't give her any reason to be confident in my ability to commit to a woman. The only thing I can do is show her.

And not just by fucking her crazy every night—I need to stay.

But I don't even worry about it, because that's the easy part. I have no intention of going anywhere. Ever.

I drive over to Selene's house and let myself in. Although she's redecorated over the years, it's still a little strange to be

Always Have

here. It probably always will be. We were kids in this house. Every inch is full of memories. Some are fantastic, particularly the ones with the three of us together. Sliding down the stairs on sheets of cardboard, hiding in the extra bedroom and jumping out to scare the girls, snuggling up on the couch with a tub of popcorn and a movie. Others are harder to face, although the sting has faded to a dull ache as the years have gone by.

I go to the garage and grab the small red toolbox that belonged to my dad. The rim is rusted and there's a dent in the side. I can still remember him opening it to find a screwdriver so he could put batteries in our toys on Christmas morning.

"Selene," I call out as I walk back to the kitchen with the tools. "Where you at?"

Her voice is faint, coming from upstairs. "Be down in a minute."

I turn on the water and flip the switch to see if the disposal turns on. Nothing. I check the drain, but I don't find anything jammed in there.

"Hey," Selene says.

"Hey sis," I say. "What did you do to this thing? Did it just stop working?"

"I didn't do anything," she says. "I don't even use it that much, but I tried this morning when I was cleaning up, and nothing happened."

"Maybe it's the circuit. I'll flip the breaker."

"I'm sorry, I should have tried that," she says. "I didn't even think of it."

I shrug. "It's no big deal."

"Hey, have you talked to Kylie?" she says.

I freeze. Selene's voice has a conspiratorial undertone, like she has a secret she wants to dangle in front of me. I retreat behind my wall, forcing my expression to stay casual. "Yeah, I guess. Why?"

"Really? Well maybe you got more out of her than I did," Selene says. "Did she tell you she broke up with Derek?"

I hope that's all the news Selene thinks there is. "Yeah, she told me."

"Did she tell you why?" Selene asks, like she already knows the answer, but wants to find out if I know.

"I don't know, she just said it wasn't working," I say.

Selene shakes her head. "I'm pretty sure she left him for someone else."

I look down at the counter. It is so hard to keep everything from showing on my face. "What makes you say that?"

She looks up at the ceiling, like she's thinking it through. "Mostly just a feeling. I talked to her earlier in the week, and she sounded different."

"Different, how?"

"Well, for one thing, I'm pretty sure I called her right after sex. I could hear it in her voice."

I search my memory, but I don't remember Kylie getting a call from Selene, particularly not right after we had sex. Although we've probably had more sex in the last week than I did in the entirety of my last relationship, so practically anytime day or night could arguably be "right after sex."

I shrug again, making a noncommittal noise, and pretend to be busy searching through the tools.

"Oh my god," Selene says.

My back and shoulders tense, but I keep my eyes on the tools, like I'm bored by Selene's conversation. "What?"

"You know something."

"I don't know what you're talking about," I say.

"Braxton," she says, her voice stern. "Tell me."

Shit. Shit. Shit. What do I say? "Tell you what?"

"Tell me what Kylie told you," she says.

"Well, if Kylie didn't tell you, maybe she didn't want you to know." Fuck. That was the wrong thing to say.

"What the hell does that mean?"

"Nothing, I'm just trying to get you off my back." I'm panicking. "Yeah, she said she dumped Derek for someone. I think it's just a fuck fling though. No big deal. That's probably why she didn't say anything. She doesn't want you to think she's crazy."

"So why did she tell *you*?" Selene asks.

"I, uh ... I saw her. She sucks at lying to my face, so I called her out."

Selene drums her fingernails along the counter top. "I guess that makes sense. She *is* a shitty liar. And I haven't seen her, so..."

"See? There you go," I say. "I'm sure it's nothing."

"Damn it, I hate it when she keeps things from me," Selene says. "Oh well. I guess I didn't tell her about Matthew right away. And after Derek, she deserves to be with someone who can push her buttons."

That sounds like something I very much want to hear. "What does that mean?"

Selene shrugs her shoulders. "He didn't really do it for her. She told me a while ago that she hadn't had a real orgasm in ages."

I turn back to the sink to hide the wide smile that crosses my face.

"Sucks for her," I say. I head toward the garage again. "I'm going to go check that breaker."

The circuit was tripped, so I flip it back. I go to the kitchen and turn on the switch. The disposal rumbles.

"There you go," I say.

"Thanks, Brax," Selene says. "Sorry I made you come

over for that."

"It's fine," I say. "But I gotta get out of here. I'll talk to you later, okay?"

"Where are you off to?" she asks. "Hot date tonight?"

I just laugh as I walk toward the door. I don't want to say anything else and dig myself in a deeper hole. Fuck fling? What the hell was I thinking with that one?

"Bye, Selene."

I shut the door behind me. I'll have to tell Kylie to go along with it until we have a chance to sit down with Selene and tell her what's really going on. Man, she's going to have my ass for this.

I'm not sure if I mean Kylie, or my sister.

19

KYLIE

How did I ever live without Braxton? Nothing has been the same since he kissed me in that restaurant booth. He saturates my existence, fills every part of me, body and soul. The days before him fade into gray, into nothing. The days since are bright, vibrant. Alive.

I'm so in love with him. I thought I might be in love a dozen times in the past, but I never was. I never knew what love really felt like until I experienced it with Brax. Now I can't imagine anything else. I can't imagine loving anyone else. Ever.

And I'm scared shitless over it. Because this is Braxton.

He loves me with fury, fucking me into oblivion, making love to me with desperate tenderness. His kisses melt me, turn my brain to mush. His touch makes me shiver and tremble. When he's inside me, when we're as close as two people can possibly get, I don't want it to end. I want to be connected to him, to have his skin against mine, his breath on my neck. I can't get enough.

I haven't slept at home once since the first night we were

together, and I'm starting to wonder if I ever will again. I hate the thought of sleeping alone, without his strong body against me. I drift through my days, a smile rarely off my face. My coworkers comment that something has changed. I shrug and smile, keeping my secret to myself.

It's harder to keep it from Selene.

Why Braxton had to tell her I'm having a fling on the side, I have no idea. He said he panicked. At this point, I'm avoiding Selene—putting her off when she asks to hang out. That's messed up, and I know it, but I'm not sure what to do about it yet. I wish Braxton had just told her the truth, but he swears it will be fine. He says he'll take the heat, and he's sure she'll understand.

Then Selene goes out of town with Matthew, so I feel like the pressure is off and I can relax—at least until she gets back.

Sunday morning, I'm cozied up on Braxton's couch, eating pancakes. Pancakes are literally my favorite food ever, and his are the best. So light and fluffy, and slathered in butter. Braxton stands in the kitchen, finishing the last batch. He's wearing nothing but dark blue boxer briefs, and if we hadn't just fucked over the side of the couch half an hour ago, I'd probably be going for his cock right now.

Because, oh my god, his cock is magnificent. It's fucking magic.

He grins at me as he flips a pancake, and I realize I'm staring at him. "How's your breakfast?" he asks.

"Amazing," I say. "Almost as amazing as you."

His smile widens and he drizzles syrup over his pancakes, then brings his plate to the couch and sits down next to me. "Are you sure they're good? You aren't eating." He raises his eyebrows.

"I'm distracted by your abs again," I say.

He looks down at himself and laughs. "They're your abs now, baby girl."

I shift so I'm facing him and tuck my toes under his leg. "You are so sexy."

"God, I love hearing you say that."

I watch him take a bite. He licks the syrup from his lips, and I start getting hot between the legs again. "How did I get so lucky?"

He puts his hand on my foot and squeezes. "I'm the lucky one." He takes another bite, then looks at me with his head tilted to the side. "Ky, what do you want to do?"

"Today?"

"No, not today," he says. "I mean, what do you dream about doing? What's on your list?"

"My list?" I take another bite, considering. "Lots of things, I guess. I want to travel. I haven't been that many places."

"Where would you go?"

"Somewhere tropical would be great. Hawaii or the Caribbean, maybe. There are lots of places in Europe that I think would be amazing to see. And there's one thing I've always dreamed of doing, but..." It seems like such a silly thing, I'm not sure I want to tell him.

"What?" He nudges my foot. "Tell me."

"I've always wanted to spend New Year's Eve in London. I want to stand under Big Ben and watch that huge clock tick over to midnight."

"Okay," he says. "Let's do it."

"What?" New Year's is three months away, and we've already been together for a month. Has Braxton ever had a relationship last that long? I try to ignore the sick feeling in my tummy when I think about that. "Are you serious?"

"Of course I'm serious," he says. "This year, it's happening. New Year's Eve in London. You and me."

I laugh. "Are you for real?"

He meets my eyes. "It's all real, baby girl. All of it."

My phone rings, and I reach to the coffee table to pick it up. It's my dad.

"Hey, Dad," I say.

"Hi, Kylie," he says. "How are you?"

"I'm great," I say, winking at Braxton. "How are you feeling today?"

"I'm all right," he says.

I can tell he isn't. His voice sounds strained.

"Let's bring him dinner later," Braxton says quietly.

I hesitate for a beat. I've seen my dad once since Braxton and I got together, but I didn't tell him about us. I was still so overwhelmed that I wasn't sure what to say. And since we haven't told Selene, I've felt like we need to hide it from the world.

But I know Dad is calling me because he's lonely, and probably in pain. I should absolutely go see him, and this could be a good time to tell him what's going on. I just don't know what he's going to think.

"Do you want to have dinner tonight?" I ask. "I'm, um ... I'm with Brax, and he and I could come over."

"That would be great," he says. "I'd like that very much."

I meet Braxton's eyes and nod. "Great. We'll bring food with us. What sounds good?"

"Whatever you want is fine," he says. He always says that.

"Okay, we'll see you later today," I say. "Love you."

"Love you too, Kylie."

I hang up and put the phone down. "So, I guess we're going to visit my dad together?"

Braxton smiles like it's the best idea in the world. "Yes, we are."

BRAXTON KEEPS his hand on the small of my back as we walk into the assisted living facility. It feels so odd for him to touch me like this in public—so familiar and intimate. Like we're a couple. Which, we are, I guess, although I feel like I'm still not sure what's happening between us. I want to believe he and I have something solid, but I have to remind myself who he is.

The woman at the front desk looks up and smiles. "Hi, Kylie," she says. "Braxton, I haven't seen you in a while. How have you been?"

"I've been absolutely fantastic, Chelsea," he says. He grabs the pen and signs in. "How about you?"

She gives him a shy smile. "Oh, I've been fine. Henry should be upstairs in his apartment. You two have a nice visit."

I look up at Braxton as we walk to the elevator. "How does she know you?"

"She's usually here when I come by," he says.

I stop in my tracks. He can't be serious. "You visit my dad?"

"Yeah, I try to visit once every week or two," he says. "I thought you knew that."

I stare at him, my mouth open. "No, I didn't. I guess, sometimes Dad says he's seen you, but I didn't know you visit him regularly."

"Of course I do," he says.

This man. I thought I knew Braxton, but I'm learning things I never would have guessed.

I follow him into the elevator, clutching a paper bag with Greek takeout. A tingle of adrenaline runs through my limbs. We get to the door and I pull out my key—I always let myself in so he doesn't have to come to the door—and take a deep breath.

I knock before opening the door. "Hi, Dad," I say as we walk in.

Dad is already at the table, a water bottle with a straw on his tray. My chest constricts. His once-dark hair is peppered with gray and, although lines crease his eyes and forehead, he doesn't look old. But he slumps forward, and his hands are twisted. He smiles, but I can see the pain in his eyes.

"Hi, Kylie," he says. "Hi, Braxton. Thanks for coming."

"Of course, Mr. Winters," Braxton says.

Dad looks back and forth between us. Braxton is still touching me on the back, but I'm not sure if Dad can see. What do I do now? Make an announcement?

Braxton drops his hand and takes the food. "Here, I'll get plates."

Dad watches us pass, and I follow Braxton into the kitchen. He starts dishing up the food. The scents of dill, paprika and lemon fill the air. He keeps his eyes on what he's doing, and something about his body language makes me anxious. He glances up, his brow furrowed, his eyes tight. He looks so tense.

Holy shit. He's nervous. I don't think I've ever seen Braxton nervous before.

I keep my voice low. "You okay?"

"Yeah, of course," he says. For a second, the tension is gone from his face and I'm sure I imagined it. But he looks out through the kitchen doorway, and I see it flash across his features again.

We take our food to the table and I set Dad's plate in

front of him. Am I imagining things, or does he keep looking between me and Braxton? We all dig into our meals. Braxton's leg brushing up against mine does nothing to alleviate my nervousness.

We make small talk for a few minutes before lapsing into silence while we eat. I finish about half of my dinner and start pushing the rest around my plate. I need to say something, but the longer the silence goes on the harder it is to speak up.

"You two are awfully quiet," Dad says. "What were you up to this morning?"

"When you called?" Braxton asks. "We were having breakfast."

I cough and almost drop my fork. "Sorry, tickle in my throat." I take a drink of water to cover.

"Breakfast together?" Dad asks. My dad isn't stupid. He stares at Braxton with one eyebrow raised.

Oh, no. He's about to unleash the lawyer.

Braxton looks at me, and a wide smile crosses his face. He tucks my hair behind my ear, then picks up my hand and kisses the backs of my fingers.

My eyes widen. I stare at Braxton, afraid to look at my dad, my heart racing.

I can see Dad in the corner of my vision. He watches us for a long moment. "Is this new?"

"Yeah, Dad it is," I say. I take my hand back from Braxton, suddenly self-conscious.

Dad's eyes move back and forth between us a few more times. "I wasn't sure I was going to live to see the day."

"What?" I ask.

"Okay, Braxton," Dad says, his lawyer voice coming back. He sets down his fork. "I thought I would have had this talk with you a long time ago, but there are a few things you need to know if you're going to date my daughter."

Braxton shifts slightly away from me.

"Dad, you don't have to—"

"Kylie," Dad says, cutting me off. "First, there's a place over in Lake City that makes her favorite blueberry pancakes."

"The Breakfast Club," Braxton says.

"Exactly," Dad says. "Good. Second, she gets grouchy if she doesn't get enough sleep, so don't keep her out too late. She's been like that since she was little."

"Dad!"

"Plenty of sleep," Braxton says, nodding. "Got it."

"Third, she might not have followed my lead in going to law school, but she learned to argue from the best. Pick your battles. Sometimes you need to let her win."

"Dad!" I say again.

Braxton smiles. I can tell he's enjoying this.

"Finally..." Dad pauses, holding Braxton's gaze. "Be good to my girl. You're like a son to me, Braxton, but if you hurt my Kylie, remember, I know all the best lawyers."

"I won't, Mr. Winters," Braxton says. He glances at me and my heart flutters. "Never."

After lunch, we go back to Braxton's place. I made it through the rest of the visit without crying, but it wasn't easy. My dad looked so happy. We said we haven't told Selene yet, and he said he'd keep it to himself if he talked to her. His eyes shone when he said goodbye to us. I haven't seen him look so relaxed in a long time.

Braxton goes into the kitchen and I sit on a stool on the other side of the counter. It's so hard seeing my dad these days, and this visit was emotionally exhausting.

"What do you need?" Braxton asks. "More pancakes?"

I laugh. "No."

"Beer?" he asks.

"Yes," I say. "Definitely beer."

He pulls two bottles out of the fridge and opens them, then hands one to me.

I take a sip. I had no idea what my dad would think of Braxton and I being together, but I certainly didn't anticipate his reaction. He said he was surprised it took us this long. How did he know? What has he been seeing all these years? And why have I been so blind to it?

And the fact that Braxton visits my dad regularly—I'm blown away. Braxton never told me, and my dad never made it clear. I stare at Brax as he pokes around in the kitchen. He turns his back to me and reaches into a cupboard to get something. There's so much about him I didn't know.

I set down my beer. "Braxton, I love you."

He freezes, his back still to me.

Oh my god. I can't believe I just said that. I blurted it out without even thinking. I'm going to freak him out. This is too much. It's too soon. Braxton doesn't go there. I don't think I've ever heard him say it, even to Selene, and I know he loves his sister. I panic, my mouth half-open. I want to backtrack, make a joke, tell him I'm not serious.

I don't want to scare him away.

In an instant, his strong arms are around me, enveloping me. He buries his face in my neck, his breath hot against my skin. I put my arms around him, and he holds me so tight it's almost hard to breathe.

He takes a shuddering breath. I wrap my arms tighter, matching the fierceness with which he clutches onto me. It's like he's drowning, and I'm the only thing keeping him above water. I caress the back of his head, running my fingers through his hair.

He pulls away just enough to look at me. "I love you so much," he says, his voice low. He presses a hand against my face. "I have wanted to say that to you for so long. I was afraid you wouldn't be able to say it back to me."

This side of him is so disarming. I never knew it existed. Tears spring to my eyes.

"Of course I love you," I say. "I've always loved you. I just didn't admit it until recently."

His lips come to mine and he kisses me, deep and slow. He's so warm and strong. My heart feels like it's swelling, like the Grinch's in that Christmas movie. It keeps growing, and I wonder if it will burst through my ribs.

He pulls back again, a sly smirk on his face. His voice is gravelly. "Now I better fuck the shit out of you so you don't question my manliness."

He picks me up and carries me to his room.

I'm caught between laughing and crying. He loves me. He feels what I feel, and what I feel is so huge I almost can't believe it. No one will ever compare to my Braxton. His skin is on mine, our bodies close. He pushes himself in deep, and I realize the truth.

I'll never want anyone else.

20

BRAXTON

I wake up early on a Sunday morning. A ray of sun peaks through the blinds, falling on Kylie's hair spread out over my pillow. God, I love this woman. I wake up to her every morning and I can't imagine anything better.

She looks so peaceful I decide not to wake her. I quietly head for the bathroom and turn on the shower. Selene has been back for a while, and we still haven't seen her—not together, at least. Kylie went to a movie with her last week, but I had a client request a late appointment, so I couldn't join them. A few days later, I went to Selene's house to help her move some furniture around, but Kylie was at work. We have plans to see her tonight and hang out, just the three of us. It's going to be such a relief to have this out in the open. I hate lying to her. She's going to be mad, but I figure I'll get a couple drinks in her before Kylie and I drop our bombshell.

The hot water flows over me as I step into the shower. I turn my face into the spray and hear the door open.

"Morning," Kylie says.

I glance through the glass door. She's naked.

Fuck, yes.

How many times have I jacked off in the shower, imagining this very thing? Seeing Kylie through the steam, all creamy skin and dark hair, her pink nipples erect. She has perfect curves—beautiful round tits, hips that swell from her narrow waist. My cock is instantly hard, just looking at her.

"Come here, baby girl," I say, opening the shower door.

She steps in and eyes my cock. "He's happy to see me."

"He's always happy to see you," I say. I slip my hands around her waist and kiss her wet lips.

She sucks water off my neck, her hands caressing down my abs, toward my very eager dick. Her teeth graze across my chest. I want to pick her up and fuck her against the shower wall, but she goes lower, her mouth working its way down.

There's no way I'm stopping this.

She gets to my lower abdomen, kissing and nibbling. I'm already breathing hard, the anticipation of her taking my cock in her mouth driving me crazy. I reach up and adjust the shower head so the spray doesn't drown her.

Kylie looks up at me, those blue-gray eyes wicked and playful. She takes the shaft in one hand and puts her lips around the crown, her eyes locked with mine.

There's nothing quite like watching a woman suck my cock, and watching Kylie do it is fucking fantastic. She holds my gaze and slowly draws me in, her mouth slick and warm. She holds the shaft, squeezing just right, and starts plunging down on me in a steady rhythm. Her head bobs up and down, taking in as much as she can. She's so good, careful with her teeth. She pulls out and sucks on the tip, then takes me in again.

I fist my hand through her wet hair and guide her. Her mouth opens wide for me, taking my girth. It's hard to hold back and I push harder. She moans into me and I move faster. She grabs the base with one hand and my ass with the other. I thrust in and out, moving my hips into her. I don't want to hurt her, but she takes it, never pulling away. In and out, her mouth hot and so wet. I hit the back of her throat, but she doesn't even flinch.

God, she feels amazing. I run my fingers through her hair with both hands, pushing my cock into her mouth, over and over, picking up the pace. I feel the first pulses and look down, meeting her eyes. I'm fucking her mouth hard, and I need to know she's okay. I loosen my grip on her hair and slow down, my dick throbbing. She looks up at me, giving me a little nod.

Her tongue swirls around the tip and she plunges down on my cock again. She sucks it like she wants it, wants me to come inside her, spill myself down her throat. I lean my head back, thrusting my hips, my body stiffening.

"Fuck, yes, Kylie. Fuck, fuck, yes."

I keep pounding into her mouth. My dick throbs, and suddenly I'm coming, pulse after pulse, unleashing into her. My body goes rigid, my legs almost buckling. Holy shit. I'm overcome, the orgasm hitting me like a fucking truck.

When I finish, Kylie stands up, licking her lips, and wipes her chin.

I wrap my arms around her and softly, carefully, kiss her mouth.

"I didn't hurt you, did I?" I ask.

"No," she says. She drags my lower lip between her teeth and takes my hand, putting it between her legs. "But now I'm so hot, you better fuck me good."

"Baby girl, I'll fuck you so good, no one else will ever compare," I say.

She meets my eyes. "I don't want anyone else, Braxton. Not ever."

"I love you so much." I grab the back of her neck and bring her mouth to mine. I kiss her hard and push two fingers into her pussy. She wasn't kidding. She's hot as fuck, ready for me. Even after that epic orgasm, my dick gets hard again, almost instantly.

Maybe I do get to fuck her against the shower wall.

I grab her ass, ready to hoist her up. "Do you want it here, baby girl? Or should we get out?"

"Here. Now."

I pick her up and she wraps her legs around my waist. I press her back into the wall, suddenly very glad I put in an extra-wide shower. I sink my cock into her, and she leans her head back.

"I need you so bad, Braxton," she says, her voice tinged with urgency.

I thrust into her, again and again, giving her what she needs. She holds on to me, her arms around my neck, her pussy so hot and tight I'm close to coming again.

"Yes, baby," she says. "Yes, fuck yes."

I love making her lose control. I hold onto her, plunging my cock in deep. She heats up, her pussy tightening around me. I almost have her.

I turn her hips up a little so her clit grinds harder against me. Her eyes widen, and she moves her face close to mine, our foreheads touching. I keep going, plunging in and out, loving her with every inch of me.

Her pussy clenches and we pause, hovering on the brink of ecstasy.

"I love you," she says.

I thrust in again and we both tumble—pulsing, hot

madness overtaking us. She calls my name and I empty inside her, losing myself completely.

We finish and I help her get her feet on the floor. The water's gone cold, so I turn up the heat.

"Fuck, Kylie, I'm undone." I wrap one hand around her waist, the other behind her head. I look deep into her eyes. "No one has ever done this to me."

She smiles and lifts up onto her toes to kiss my mouth. "No one else ever will."

I know, with every ounce of my being, that she's right.

WE SHOW up together at Brody's, and I have to remind myself not to touch her. She looks hot as hell in a snug blue t-shirt and tight jeans. Her ass is ridiculous. I want to grab it, but I see my sister in a booth and keep it under control.

As soon as I see Selene's face, I know something is wrong. She doesn't meet my eyes and she's fiddling with her bracelet, chewing on her lower lip. There's a tightness around her eyes.

But more than that, I can feel it. I can feel how upset she is. I sit down across from her, wondering if this is about Kylie.

Kylie slides in next to her. "Hey, Selene. What's going on?"

"Fucking Matthew," Selene says.

My back and shoulders tense.

"What happened?" Kylie asks.

"He dumped me this morning."

Anger sears through me and I clench my fists.

"What?" Kylie says. "You're kidding."

Selene shakes her head and bites her lip. I can tell she's

trying not to cry. "No, I'm serious." She takes a shaky breath. "Why do I do this to myself? Every guy I date is just like him, some wannabe player with a hot body and a bank account. I have my own fucking bank account, so why do I always end up with these men who think their money excuses all their bullshit?"

"What did he say?" Kylie asks. "You guys just went to Mexico. What's up with that?"

Selene takes a sip of her drink. "I have no clue. He didn't give a reason. He didn't even tell me in person. He texted first, but I called him. Who the hell breaks up with someone with a fucking text?"

I shift uncomfortably in my seat. I've definitely done that.

Selene sniffs. "I knew things weren't going well before we went to Mexico, but we had such a great time when we were away. I don't know what happened."

Kylie puts her arm around Selene and meets my eyes. She shakes her head, just enough that I can see. We can't tell Selene. Not right now.

I want to smash that Matthew bastard's goddamn head into a wall. I knew he was going to do this to her; I could tell the first time I met him. He wasn't serious about her.

He was too much like me. At least, the me before Kylie.

Not that there was anything I could do about it. Kylie and I danced around the subject of each other's relationships, but Selene just gets pissed when I try to tell her the guy she's dating is an asshole. Even if I can spot them a fucking mile away.

I let the girls chat a bit longer while I calm down. I don't trust myself to talk yet. I get so angry when Selene is hurt. I want to break something. She's keeping it together pretty well, but I can feel her distress. I wish she'd quit dating these smug assholes who always leave her.

"I need to get my mind off this," Selene says. She straightens and swipes her fingers beneath her eyes. "I'm sick of being a crybaby over these dipshits. Fuck them. Let's talk about something else. What's up with your guy, Kylie? When do we get to meet the man who beat out Derek Marshall?"

Kylie's eyes widen with alarm and it's all I can do not to let a smug smile cross my face.

Fuck yeah, I beat out Derek Marshall.

"Oh, right," Kylie says. "No, that's not really anything. It's no big deal."

"Come on, Kylie, give me something," Selene says. "What? Is he, like, dumb as a rock with a big dick? Is that why we can't meet him?"

Kylie laughs, meeting my eyes. "Yeah, huge. The sex is off the charts."

I have to stop myself from smiling again.

"Good for you, babe. One of us should be getting some." Selene's eyes move to me. "You're being quiet."

You're mad. Focus on mad. "I want to punch Matthew in the teeth."

Selene sighs and leans her head on Kylie's shoulder. "I know. I should just let you at him."

"Selene, you need to adjust your standards," Kylie says. "Take some time for you, but when you're ready to get back in the game, quit with the pretty boys. Find someone different."

"Hey, you committed to different, and you wound up with a fuck fling you won't introduce to your friends."

"Yeah, but, that's ... different," Kylie says. "He's different for me."

"Don't get me wrong, I'm not judging," Selene says. "Have your fun, girl. And I know you're right. I'm such a sucker for the wrong men."

"What do you need?" Kylie asks. "Wanna go back to your house and drink?"

"Yeah, but I think I want fries first," she says.

"Atta girl," Kylie says, and rubs her hand across Selene's back.

Kylie meets my eyes again and gives me a tight-lipped smile.

As much as I want to tell Selene what's going on, it doesn't feel right. Tonight, she needs us. And I always give my sister what she needs.

21

KYLIE

A new song comes on and people cheer—*Monster Mash*. We've been listening to a steady stream of cheesy Halloween music, but I guess it fits. Selene decided to go all-out and throw a huge Halloween party, and she's definitely outdone herself. She brought in a decorator to transform her house into a mass of black sheets, pumpkins, ghosts, spider webs, and twinkling orange and purple lights. She even hired a guy to bartend. He's dressed like a zombie doctor, with some very convincing makeup, but his drinks are damn good.

Everyone is in costume. I think half the women went to the same section at the costume store—I see a sexy nurse, sexy cop, sexy French maid (although, is there any other kind?), sexy librarian. Some tall chick I don't know is a Playboy bunny. The guys are dressed up as everything from superheroes and vampires to a dude in a scary clown costume who I wish would just leave already.

I fucking hate clowns.

I went all-out, too, with an old-school Wonder Woman costume. I'm not really tall enough, but I do have the long, dark hair. And hell, my boobs look amazing in this thing. I have the strapless bodysuit, knee high boots, and I even have a gold whip tied at my hip. It's kind of kinky. I picked it because Braxton will be here, and he'll have to look at me in this thing all night—without touching me.

Of course, my plan to spend the evening teasing him would work a lot better if he were actually here.

I know he's coming. I saw him a few hours ago. But I went back to my apartment to change so he wouldn't see my costume before the party. I've been here for a while, sipping a weird purple drink that's dangerously good, and I haven't seen any sign of him.

Selene is rocking a smoking hot witch getup, with a tiny black skirt that shows off her crazy long legs, and a corset with a sparkling silver spider webs all over it. Her lips are deep red, and she has long false eyelashes that make her look pretty wicked. She's hanging out with a few people she must know from work, because I'm not sure who they are. It's good to see her having fun. She bounced back from Matthew pretty well—I think it helped that she knew the end was coming. I hope she listens to me and tries to find a guy who isn't such a player next time. Selene's fucking amazing—she deserves someone great.

A wave seems to ripple through the party and I glance toward the front door to see what's going on. People step aside, and in walks Braxton.

That fucker. He totally one-upped me.

He's dressed as *Magic Mike*, wearing nothing but a pair of jeans and a tie, showing off his broad chest and rippling abs. His skin glistens, and his jeans sit low, revealing the top of that delicious V.

I clench my thighs together against the rush of heat. My panties are instantly drenched.

At least half the party stares at him. The Playboy Bunny girl almost drops her drink, her mouth hanging open. Even the guy she was talking to watches him open-mouthed. Braxton catches my eye, one corner of his mouth turning up in a smirk.

I'm going to kill him.

I make a show of looking away, and take a sip of my drink. I watch him from the corner of my eye. He says hi to a few people, making his way toward his sister.

Selene points at him and laughs when she catches sight of him. He goes in to hug her and she balks, pushing him away.

"Hey, looks like we belong together."

I turn to find a guy in a Superman costume smiling at me.

"What?"

"Wonder Woman," he says, gesturing at my costume.

"Oh, right, Superman," I say.

"That's a great look on you," he says.

Uh-oh. I didn't even think about what to do if a guy hit on me. Brax and I are still on the down-low, and we're not about to go public in the middle of Selene's party. I glance in Braxton's direction, but he's still talking to Selene.

"Thanks," I say, looking away so I don't appear interested.

"Can I get you another drink?" he asks.

"Oh, no thanks, I'm good." I hold up my half-full cup.

He steps closer. "I'm Paul. Care to give up your secret identity?"

Man of Steel here is not getting the hint, but I don't want to be rude. "Kylie."

"It's very nice to meet you, Kylie," he says. He holds out a hand and I take it. He starts to shake, then brings the backs of my fingers up to his lips and kisses my hand.

I snatch my hand back. "Paul, it's very nice to meet you, but—"

Paul's eyes widen, and I stop mid-sentence. Someone is suddenly standing very close behind me, and I don't have to turn around to know who it is.

"Hey, Kylie," Braxton says. His hand brushes my ass and I try not to gasp. He's standing so close that I feel a little dizzy.

"Hi, Braxton," I say, barely resisting the urge to run my hands all over his abs.

Braxton shifts so he's next to me and stares at my boobs, making zero attempt to hide what he's doing. "Holy shit, you look hot as fuck in that thing."

My mouth drops open. Does he not remember we're supposed to keep this quiet?

"Um, wow," Paul says. "Kylie and I were having a conversation here."

Braxton looks over at Paul, then back at me. "Shit, I can't compete with Superman. You two have fun." He quirks an eyebrow at me and saunters away.

I watch him go, my mouth still hanging open.

"Who the fuck was that guy?" Paul says.

I can't stop staring at Braxton's ass in those jeans. "What? Oh, that's Braxton. He's Selene's brother."

"Kind of a dick, isn't he?" Paul asks.

I laugh, my eyes still on Brax. "You have no idea."

Paul looks back and forth between Braxton and me a couple of times, then shakes his head and walks away.

A girl in a purple genie costume walks up to Braxton. I take a sip of my drink, trying to pretend like I'm not watching them. He smiles at her, but angles his body away when she tries to move closer. His eyes dart to me and I arch one eyebrow. His shoulders tense up, and he rubs the back of his neck. He shoots another quick glance in my direction.

Oh, this is fantastic. He actually looks uncomfortable.

The girl reaches out to touch his arm, a classic flirty move, and he flinches. Under different circumstances, I'd be pissed, but I know he wore that so-called costume to torture me, so I love that it's backfiring on him.

Selene sidles up next to me and slips her arm through mine.

"Having fun?" she asks.

I blink, trying to act like I wasn't just staring at her brother. "Yeah, this is a great party. The decor is fantastic."

"Thanks," she says. "I'd take credit, but I just paid a guy to do it for me. It does look pretty amazing, though. I should do this every year."

"Definitely," I say.

"God, look at him," Selene says, gesturing toward Braxton. He's still talking to the genie girl, and two others linger nearby. "He's such an attention whore."

"Yeah, he is."

"I wonder which one of those poor girls he's going to hook up with tonight," Selene says. "Although it almost seems like he's been going through a dry spell lately. No, that's probably my imagination. He never goes through dry spells."

Nope, definitely not a dry spell. I try to sound uninterested. "Who knows?"

"What do women see in him, anyway?" she asks.

I really wish we weren't discussing him like this. "Well, he's your brother, so you just don't see him that way."

"I guess," she says. "So, still seeing the dumb guy with the big dick?"

I laugh. "Um, I don't know. Maybe? I guess?"

Selene looks at me and I almost blurt it out. *I'm with your brother and I love him!*

"Hey, Tina is here! I have to go say hi." She flits off in her stilettos.

I blow out a breath. That was close.

I wander around for a while, chatting with people I know. These purple drinks go down so easy, I have a couple more. Braxton circles opposite me, always keeping distance between us. He meets my eyes and winks once in a while, but he doesn't come near. The women of the party never let up, a new one darting in to talk to him every time another walks away. If he wanted attention, he's certainly getting it. It's weird to see girls flirt with him so openly without feeling the least bit jealous. They don't know he's mine, but I sure do.

And by the looks he keeps giving me, so does he.

After a while, I take my empty cup back to the makeshift bar in the kitchen. Zombie Doctor guy asks if I want another purple thing, but I grab an ice water and take a few sips. I need to hydrate or I'm going to regret it tomorrow.

Out of nowhere, Braxton appears next to me. We both stand against the island, facing out toward the rest of the party.

He leans down to speak quietly in my ear. "I don't know how much longer I can look at you dressed like that. Did you do that on purpose?"

Tingles run down my spine and I look him up and down. "Yes, but yours is worse."

He cracks a smile. "I don't know about that. Those magnificent tits of yours are driving me crazy."

I start feeling flushed, and I take another sip of water.

"Look at you. Every woman in this place wants to fuck your brains out."

He kisses my neck, right below my ear. "I only want you, baby girl."

"Brax, quit it, someone will see."

"Selene went outside." He kisses my neck again and nips my ear with his teeth. He tugs on the lasso at my hip. "I want to tie you up with this and fuck you until you can't breathe."

I take a deep breath, my pussy throbbing. "We're at a party, Brax."

"I need you, Ky," he says into my ear, his voice rough. "I need you right fucking now."

I'm about to suggest we get out of here and go back to his place, but I don't think I can wait. "Where?"

"My room."

"Selene blocked off the stairs with decorations," I say.

"Garage," he growls. "I'll go first. Meet me in sixty seconds."

I wait near the kitchen, my heart hammering. Braxton walks away, heading toward the door to the garage. It's near the front entrance, the door itself around a corner and out of sight of this side of the house. The girl in the nurse costume stops him, but he extricates himself pretty quickly. He disappears around the corner and I count to sixty, my eyes flicking around, looking for signs of anyone who might notice me heading in the same direction.

Selene comes in from the back deck, and I duck past the other guests before she sees me. No one is in the front entryway, so I open the door leading into the garage and slip through.

He's waiting for me just inside. He pushes the door shut and we're drenched in darkness.

"God, it's so hard to keep my hands off you," he says,

pushing me up against the door. He kisses down my neck and slips a hand into my bodysuit, cupping my breast.

I run my hands up and down his chest and abs, feeling the hard edges of his muscle. "This is really unfair to the rest of humanity. No one should be this perfect."

Braxton's mouth comes to mine and he overpowers me with his kiss. All thought flees. There's nothing left but his lips and tongue, his body pressing against me. His hand grips the back of my neck, firm but gentle, and he devours me.

I'm entirely his.

Braxton yanks on the Velcro on the back of my costume, ripping it off.

"This door doesn't lock," I say breathlessly. "What if someone comes in?"

"They won't."

I can't see a thing. I kick off my costume, dropping the whip with it, and pull off my thong. I'm panting, desperate for him. I hear his zipper, and the next thing I know he's holding me up, pressing my back against the cold door. I wrap my legs around him and he drives his cock inside me.

As soon as our bodies lock together, I feel whole. He pauses, holding me tight, his cock buried in my pussy. His breath is hot on my neck.

I love needing him so much. I would have fucked him in the bathroom or a closet if I had to. I love the way he fills me, unmakes me. I'm floating in bliss, high on the feel of his body melding with mine.

I don't ever want it to end.

In the darkness, every sensation is heightened. He takes out the tension of the evening on me, fucking me relentlessly. Like he needs to show me, again, what he feels. How hungry he is for me. How desperately he needs me.

The music thumps through the door, drowning us out. I breathe his name, my mouth close to his ear, and dig my fingers into his back. He feels so good, I'm delirious, drunk on his love. We come together, our bodies stiffening, shuddering. It's almost too much.

He lowers me to the floor, but doesn't let go, holding me tight against him. He kisses my neck, my jaw, finds my lips. His tongue caresses mine, soft and slow. I keep my arms around his neck, my body pressed against him.

Finally, he pulls away. "Better?" I ask.

"For now," he says, his voice throaty and low.

I laugh. "Is there a light? I don't know where the costume went."

Braxton flicks a light switch and I squint against the sudden glare. We must be quite a sight: Brax with his pants around his ankles, his chest glistening. Me dressed in nothing but red-and-gold knee-high boots.

"Oh, shit," he says with a laugh, as he pulls up his pants.

"What?"

He puts his hand along my cheek and pulls me in for another deep kiss. "You're a mess. You look like you just got fucked."

I grab my costume off the floor. He finds a package of paper towels on a shelf and helps me clean up before I put the bodysuit back on. I do my best to smooth down my hair, but I'm sure my cheeks are flushed. If Selene corners me, I guess I can blame drinking too much.

Although I smell like Braxton.

"You first," he says with a smile when we're both more or less put back together. "But I'm leaving in two minutes, tops. I want you back at my place as soon as you can get away."

I lift onto my tiptoes to kiss him again. "I'll be out of here in three."

I slip through the door, into the entry foyer, and walk back to the party. I find Selene and let her know I'm tired and heading home. She tries to talk me into staying in my room here, but she's distracted by another friend, so I don't have to come up with an excuse. I give her a quick hug goodbye and leave through the front door.

Braxton is waiting just outside. Although he's shirtless and it's a freezing October night, he puts his coat around my shoulders. He takes my hand in his, twining our fingers together, and we walk back to his condo in silence.

22

BRAXTON

"That ought to do it," I say, turning the wrench one more time. Selene's kitchen sink was leaking, so I came over between clients to take a look. "It just needed a little tightening."

I get up and brush my hands together.

"Thanks," she says. "Do you have time to stay for lunch?"

"Depends," I say. "Are you cooking?"

She glares at me. "I can cook."

I raise an eyebrow at her.

She rolls her eyes and gets a bag out of the fridge. "Fine. I grabbed sandwiches before you got here."

She sets out our lunch on the island and we both pull up a barstool.

"Do you think Mom and Dad would have kept this place?" she asks out of the blue. "You know, if they were still around."

I put my sandwich down. "Yeah, I think they would have. This is a great old house."

"I just wonder. Life would be so different. Would we still

live so close? Would they have us over for dinner?" She pauses for a moment. "Sorry, I know it's hard to talk about them."

It is hard to talk about them, but I don't want her to feel like she can't. "It's okay, I don't mind remembering them sometimes. You can talk to me about whatever you want."

She nudges me with her elbow. "Thanks, Brax. You're a good guy, you know that?"

I feel a twinge of guilt, and shrug. Maybe I should just tell her about Kylie. But I know Kylie wants to be here when I do, and she's at work. "Hey, we should do a movie night. Just the three of us."

"Sure," Selene says. "If you can get Kylie to come."

"Why wouldn't she come?" I ask.

"Well, she's been banging some guy for who knows how long and won't introduce me, so..."

Even though I know the guy is me, a jolt of jealousy rams itself into my gut. *Calm down, dumbass.* I force my face to stillness, but I know Selene saw my expression change. She's looking at me with too much scrutiny.

The stab of jealousy turns into a swarm of guilt. I never should have lied to her.

"So, what about you?" she asks. "You haven't said a word about a girl in months. Who are you sleeping with these days?"

"God, Selene, why would you even ask me that? I don't want to know if you're sleeping with someone."

She shrugs. "I don't know. You seem like you're busy all the time. I figure there must be a girl involved."

How should I play this? I don't want to play it at all anymore. I'm sick of hiding my relationship with Kylie. It was a stupid thing to do in the first place, and I want it to be over. But I have to tread carefully. I promised myself a long time ago that I wouldn't hurt my sister. Losing Mom and Dad almost killed her, and I couldn't live with myself if I caused her pain.

Of course, I've been lying to her about Kylie for months. Isn't that going to cause her pain?

No, it's going to make her mad, and I can deal with mad Selene.

"Yeah, there might be someone," I say.

"Do you want to tell me about her?" she asks.

There's something weird in her voice. First of all, since when does she care who I'm seeing, especially if I'm just having a fling on the side with someone I don't intend to bring around? It wouldn't be the first time, not by a long shot. Second, she sounds too suspicious. Like she knows what's going on and she's trying to get me to admit it.

Fuck.

"Why do you want to know?" I ask, shooting her an annoyed look.

She shrugs again. "Just wondering."

She picks up her sandwich, but she stares straight ahead into the kitchen. I can tell she's thinking about something. After a lengthy silence, she puts down her food.

"I see the way you look at her," she says, her voice unusually soft.

My chest clenches. "Look at who?"

"Kylie."

I try to laugh it off, like she must be joking. "What does that mean?"

"You can't look at her like that, Brax," she says.

She's not joking. Shit. I get up and go to the fridge so she won't see my face. "I don't look at her like anything."

"Yes, you do."

She's right. No matter how hard I try to hide my feelings

when the three of us are together—which isn't very often these days, and I realize how fucked up that is—I know it still shows.

I decide to feel this out. "So what if I do?"

"No, Braxton," she says.

I look at her over my shoulder. Her face is severe.

"What do you mean, *no*?"

"You heard me," she says. "You cannot look at Kylie like that. Not ever. Do you understand me?"

Shit. My heart starts to beat too fast and adrenaline runs through my veins. What the fuck do I say now? "What are you worried about?"

"I'm worried about you. And her," she says. "And you being you. Kylie is not on the menu, Brax. You have to keep her in the friend zone."

Too late for that. "Where is this even coming from?"

"The three of us are fragile," she says. "We've known her so long, it seems like we'll all be friends forever. It's hard to imagine it any other way. But a guy-girl friendship is always breakable, *especially* when the guy is you. So whatever thing you're doing in your head where you think you can make something work out with her, you need to stop. Now. Right this second. Because if you hook up with Kylie, it will absolutely fucking kill me."

It's like my lungs are caught in a vice. I'm panicking; I can't breathe. My head is spinning, but I keep my expression still so it won't show. Hide behind my walls. I'm pretty good at maintaining a tough exterior, especially in front of Selene. I've always had to. But this has me crumbling inside, reality crashing down on me like shards of broken glass.

No. There has to be another way.

"Kill you? That's a little dramatic, don't you think?"

Her eyes are huge, and her stress and fear pours into me,

like it's my own. I can feel it, hard edged and biting. The twin thing again.

"No, it's not dramatic," she says. "Don't do it. I could not handle it if you hooked up with her. Do you understand me? You can't. Promise me."

"What?"

"Promise me you won't hook up with Kylie."

I stare at her, the rawness of her emotions pouring over me. She's totally and completely serious.

No, Selene. Please don't make me do this. Please don't make me give her up.

"Come on, Brax," she says.

She needs this from me, as much as she's ever needed anything. And I always give my sister what she needs. I run a hand through my hair to give myself a second before I have to speak, then croak out a reply: "Sure, Selene. Whatever. It's not like that. Kylie's my best friend."

"Promise," she says.

I swallow hard. "I promise."

Her shoulders relax and her expression softens. "Okay, good."

I need to get out of here. Now. "I have clients this afternoon. I have to head out."

"Okay, so movie night this weekend?" she asks.

"Sure."

Somehow I make it outside to my car. I'm surprised I'm still on my feet. Shouldn't I have dropped to the ground by now? Isn't that what happens when your heart stops beating? The blood quits flowing and your brain is starved for oxygen and you die.

How am I still alive?

I can't hurt Selene. I've been running interference for her since we were kids, standing in the way of anything that threatens her. Sometimes things get by me, especially where her relationships are concerned. I know I can't protect her from everything, and fuck, she has horrible taste in men. When she gets hurt, I deal with it with alcohol and sex, and whispered threats if I'm lucky enough to run into the bastard who messed with her.

But never me. I'm never the one doing the hurting, and I never will be. I guard her with my life. I'd take a bullet for her—give her a kidney or a lung or my fucking heart if hers stopped working.

I certainly don't need mine anymore.

I've made two real promises in my life. One was at our parents' funeral. I didn't cry that day, even though I was ten and no one would have blamed me. I didn't cry because Selene needed to, and she needed me to be strong for her. I held her tight as we stood by their graves and I whispered my promise. *I will never hurt you. I will always take care of you.*

And I have. I've never broken that promise.

The second promise was when I told Kylie I wouldn't break her.

My two promises are colliding. There's no way I can keep them both. I can't stay with Kylie without hurting Selene. I heard it from her own lips, saw the truth of it in her face.

I can't do that to her.

My only hope left is Kylie's strength. Knowing what I have to do makes me feel like I'm drowning, but I cling to the thought that Kylie can take it. I'll explain, and maybe she'll understand.

And then I imagine her face when I tell her it's because of Selene—that Selene doesn't want us to be together, that she needs the dynamic of our friendship to stay the same.

That I'm faced with the impossible, and there's nothing else I can do. That Kylie has my heart and always will, but I'll give it up for my sister if I have to.

I can't tell Ky. She'll be angry with Selene. Of course she will. She'll blame her, and I'll do the very thing I'm trying to avoid: ruin Selene's friendship with Kylie.

And Selene will never forgive me.

I head back to the gym, but I'm going to call my clients and cancel. I can't deal with anyone right now. I'll get in a hard workout, and at some point I'll go home. Kylie will be there. And I'll have to tell her.

I'll have to be the man she was afraid I'd be.

23

KYLIE

The sound of the front door wakes me up. I got home from work late, but Braxton wasn't here, and I didn't have any messages. I tried to call, but he didn't answer, so I texted. He replied, saying he was working late. I curled up on the couch with the TV on, and must have dozed off.

He comes in and sets his keys down on the counter.

"Hey," I say, rubbing my eyes. "What time is it?"

"I don't know."

I shift so I can see the clock. It's after eleven.

"Wow, it's late," I say. "Are you okay?"

"Yeah." He heads into the kitchen and opens the fridge.

My shoulders tense up. He is not okay. "Are you sure?" I ask. I sit up and pull a pillow into my lap. Something about his posture makes me nervous.

He grabs a beer and opens it, but doesn't look at me. "Yeah."

My heart beats faster and my hands tingle, like my body is getting ready to flee. "Where were you?"

"Nowhere. Just getting a drink." He takes a long pull from the bottle.

"Okay," I say. "Did something happen? You seem upset."

"No," he says. He still won't look at me. "I just needed to do some thinking."

"About what?"

He doesn't answer, his eyes on the counter in front of him.

Something is very wrong.

My throat feels like it's closing and I almost can't speak. "Brax, what's going on?"

He's silent for a long moment. He takes another drink and sets the bottle down. "I think we made a mistake."

"What did you say?"

"This," he says. "It was a mistake. We were better off as friends."

Oh, no. No, he can't be saying this. "What are you talking about?"

He rubs his chin. "I don't think I'm cut out for this serious relationship stuff. I thought I could be, but I was wrong."

I feel sick to my stomach. I'm falling, spiraling down through nothing. Why is he doing this?

Oh, god. There's only one reason he'd do this to me out of the blue. "Holy shit, did you—" I don't know if I can say it. "Did you cheat on me?"

He finally looks up. "No. God, no."

"Then what is this about?"

He takes a deep breath. "We were great as friends—you, me, and Selene. And I screwed that up. I shouldn't have. We should have stayed the way we were. I'm no good at this stuff, Kylie. It was better before."

I stand up and wrap my arms around myself. "You can't

be serious. Are you ending this? Are you breaking up with me?"

"I think it's for the best," he says.

I stare at him, my mouth open. Tears sting my eyes. My legs shake. I'm not sure if I can stay on my feet. My bottom lip trembles and I cover my mouth with my hand. I think I might vomit. "No," I say. "No, Braxton. You can't. I thought we—"

I stop and turn away from him. A sob breaks through, shaking my shoulders. The world is crumbling around me, crashing down, leaving nothing but ruins. My body hurts, like I've been hit by a truck. He can't be doing this to me. He said he wouldn't. He *promised* he wouldn't break me.

I close my eyes. He'll only break me if I let him. I feel like I'm being ripped to shreds, but fuck if I'm going to fall apart here, in front of him.

Goddammit, I should have known. This is *Braxton*. How else did I think this was going to end? I saw the end play out as soon as it began.

I slowly lower my hand and take a deep breath, swallowing back the panic that tries to rise in my throat. I clench my teeth together, anger burning through my veins. "This is my fault," I say. My voice is cold, unemotional.

"What?" he asks.

I shake my head. "I should have known better. I was stupid enough to think I was special. That I was different. God, I was such an idiot. After all those women. I know you. I know who you are, and I know exactly what you do. I actually thought I could be the one to tame you."

Braxton doesn't answer.

I put a hand to my forehead. "I fell for it all. I can't believe I did that. You, Braxton Taylor, confessed your long-time love for me, and I actually thought it was real." I look up at him, stare him straight in the eyes. "You don't know what that means. You don't know what love is. You don't have a fucking clue."

"Kylie—"

"No," I say. "You want to do this? You want to break it off? Fine. But don't try to tell me it wasn't all bullshit. You owe me at least that much. You can be fucking honest with me at this point."

"Fuck, I don't know what else to do," he says.

"What is this about?" I ask. "Because this morning, when you were screwing me in your bed, you didn't seem to have such a crisis. But then, you were fucking me, so of course you didn't. Your dick was happy, and that's all that matters to you."

"That isn't true."

"Oh, really?" I'm halfway between screaming at him and crying my eyes out, and the heady swirl of emotions just makes me angrier. "Fuck you, Braxton. How dare you. How dare you touch me. It was a mistake? Fuck yes, it was a mistake. It was the biggest mistake of your life."

"Baby—"

"Don't you dare," I say, my voice sharp. "You do not get to call me that. If you're done with me, you do not have the right to talk to me that way."

I can't look at him anymore. I stomp off to his room and try to gather up my things. There's too much. I practically moved in. Why the fuck did I do that? He never asked me to. He never said we should take this to the next level and live together. I just stayed, like a stupid puppy. God, I was such an idiot.

I pull out a duffel bag and start throwing things in. He better not come in here, or I'm going to punch him in the mouth. No wonder he didn't tell Selene. This whole time, I let myself believe it was because this was so big, he didn't want to freak her out. But then he kept putting it off.

I should have known. He didn't bother telling her because he knew she'd be mad, and there was no point in pissing her off when he was just going to fuck me for a while and move on. Just like every other woman he's ever had.

I fill the bag and toss in some of my stuff from the bathroom. I'm going to have to come back at some point to get the rest. Or just leave it and never get it back. That's feeling like a better option, because I do not want to see him again. Ever. I don't think I can take it.

My keys and phone are in the living room, so I have to go back in before I can leave. Braxton is still standing in the kitchen, unmoving. I don't look at his face. I can't. I pick up my stuff and head for the front door.

"Kylie."

I pause with my hand on the doorknob, my bag slung over one shoulder.

"Please, I—"

"No," I say. "You're done. I'm leaving. And if you ever cared about me as anything more than a goddamn sex toy, you'll leave me alone. I don't *ever* want to see you again."

I pull open the door and walk out, slamming the door behind me.

I make it to the car before I break down, tossing my bag onto the passenger seat and falling forward onto the steering wheel. My body shakes; sobs choke me. I can't breathe. Part of me wants him to run after me—to come out and get in my car and tell me he was wrong. That he didn't mean it and will I please come back inside.

But I know he won't. He did mean it. He wouldn't have said it otherwise.

I cry uncontrollably, until my chest hurts and my back is

clenched and tight. I feel so lost, so hopeless. He was my world. I loved him with a fierceness that took my breath away, and it was all for nothing.

I take a few shaking breaths to calm down so I can drive home. I need to get out of here. I wipe my face with my sleeve and turn on my car. I want to go to Selene's house and melt into a puddle in her arms, but I can't. She never knew about us, and now she never will. Because fuck if I'm going to admit that I fell for it—that I was stupid enough to fall for him.

24

BRAXTON

The best part about love was the high. I rode it all the way to the fucking sky, soaring above the world. Until I had Kylie, I don't think I was ever really happy. I had happy moments, but they were brief and fleeting. With her, I lived each day filled with contentment—the sort of feeling that makes the rush of a hookup, the burn of whiskey, the adrenaline surge of doing something crazy all seem pointless. Those were quick hits that faded almost immediately. Kylie was steady. She made me feel open, like I could finally break down the walls and be who I am with another person.

The crash, though. The crash is killing me.

It was like jumping out of a plane with no parachute—on purpose. The free fall lasted for days. I spun out of control, no idea which way was up or down. I worked out like a maniac, got drunk as fuck, but nothing helped. I just fell, plummeting through the air, knowing I was going to hit the ground, not sure if I'd survive. Or if I wanted to.

Then I hit the dirt. I got home one night and fell into bed, still dressed. I couldn't move. I spent two days barely functioning. I canceled my appointments, turned off my phone, and let myself drown.

When I turned my phone back on, I knew I wouldn't have any messages from her. It still hurt like a kick to the gut to see that I didn't.

Eventually, I got my shit together. I went back to work. I put in extra hours at the gym. I saw my sister. I kept it all in, clawing my way to a new normal.

Because this is life, now. Life without her.

No matter how hard I try, I can't get her face out of my mind. The way she looked at me that night—so angry. I expected her to be hurt. I steeled myself to see her cry. In some fucked-up version of it, I think I even imagined holding her, being the one to soothe the pain, even though I was the asshole causing it. I wasn't prepared for such rage.

I'm well aware of how royally I fucked things up, but at this point there's nothing more I can do about it. I just have to get used to this hollow ache in my chest.

I sit at the bar, staring at my glass of Jameson. I hung out at home for a while after work, but it was too damn quiet. I didn't even think about where I was going, just took a walk and found myself here.

I glance over at the two blondes sitting nearby. It's Friday night, and the place is busy, but these two stand out. They're not here with anyone else, and they're both dressed like they mean business. Low-cut shirts, tight skirts showing a lot of leg. It's after one, and their shimmery makeup tells me they probably started out clubbing.

They've been watching me for the last ten minutes.

There are several shot glasses in front of each of them, although they've been sipping water since I got here. They cast obvious glances at me, looking me up and down. Then they lean toward each other and talk quietly, smiling and laughing.

I could probably have both if I wanted.

They have that look. The one that says *I'm in the mood to do something fucking crazy tonight*. I could go over to their table, and in five minutes have both walking out the door with me, one on each arm.

I've never done it before. A threesome would be uncharted territory for me. I'd act confident, like I have so many women throwing themselves at me, I do it all the time. Like I'm so fucking incredible, they all have to share. And I'm sure I'd make it work. I'd lose myself in their skin, their tits, their pussies. For a little while, they'd make me forget.

"Hi."

I saw them coming and didn't turn. I've given them nothing—no eye contact, no sly smile. Apparently I didn't need to.

I take a sip of my drink. "Evening."

"I'm sorry to bother you," one of them says, the smell of tequila coming off her. "I'm Amy. Sabrina and I couldn't help but notice you've been sitting here all by yourself."

I nod, still not quite looking at them. "Yeah."

Amy lifts her ass up onto the barstool next to me and slides on, crossing her legs. Sabrina stands next to her, chewing on her lower lip.

"Do you want some company?" Amy asks.

I take a deep breath. Do I? I've felt like shit for weeks, and nothing helps. It would be nice to feel something else, even though I know it won't last. I look at Amy out of the corner of my eye. She licks her lips, a smile tugging at the corners of her mouth.

I buy time by taking another drink.

"In case we're not being clear," Amy says, leaning close,

her voice sultry and low, "Sabrina and I would *both* like to know if you want company tonight."

I swallow. They're not looking for emotion—no truth, no expectations. Just sex. Just a wild and crazy experience with some guy they don't know. I could take them home, fuck them both to pieces, and send them on their way. It would be everything they're looking for. No one else would have to know.

I'd know.

"Amy," I say, finally turning toward her. Straight blond hair frames her face, and her thick eye shadow sparkles, even in the dim light. Her lips have a hint of bright pink lipstick; the rest probably rubbed off on the glasses of all the drinks she's had. Her eyes aren't quite focused. "I love that you came over here to talk to me. That was really brave. But, as tempting as you are..." I look her up and down, like I'm enjoying what I see, then do the same to Sabrina. "I'm afraid I have to decline."

Sabrina instantly looks dejected. Damn it. I was trying to let them down easy.

Amy doesn't seem to want to give up. She tilts her head and brushes her hair behind her shoulder. "Are you sure?" She trails a finger up my arm.

I look her in the eyes, holding her gaze for a long moment, and she freezes. "I'm sorry, Amy, but I can't. My heart belongs to someone else, and I can't do that to her."

Their expressions instantly change—eyebrows drawn in, little frowns crossing their mouths.

"Aw," Amy says. "You look so sad."

I toss back the rest of my drink and stand. "Yeah, well, I deserve it. Can I get a cab for you? I'd like to make sure you get home safe."

They look at each other, and Amy answers. "No, I don't think we're ready to call it yet."

I smile at both of them. "Have a good night, then, ladies. It was very nice meeting you."

I set my glass down on the bar and walk out the door without looking back.

25

KYLIE

The smell of food fills my car. I haven't had much of an appetite, but I have to admit, it's making me hungry. I picked up a turkey dinner for two from Metro Market—sliced turkey breast, stuffing, green bean casserole, butter rolls, and two slices of pumpkin pie. In the past, I've cooked for Dad on Thanksgiving, but I didn't have the energy for it this year. It's all I can do to get a takeout version and bring it to his place.

He suggested we just have dinner in his building's cafeteria, but that would mean sitting in a room with other people. I haven't seen my dad since everything blew up in my face with Braxton, and I don't know how I'm going to tell him. If I fall apart—and there's a very good chance I will—I don't need a bunch of witnesses.

I can't get that horrible night out of my mind. I still don't know what happened to flip Braxton's switch. That morning, he was fine. More than fine. He was all kisses and whispered I love yous. Of course, he had his cock in me five minutes after we woke up, so there's that. Apparently he spent the last several months thinking with his dick, and when his brain caught up he freaked out.

What I don't understand is *why*. Why did this happen?

He denied cheating on me, and despite how hurt I am, I believe him. He's always been a player, but he's never been a cheater. Did things simply get too intense? Or is this just how he operates? He has his fun and moves on. I've never seen the dynamics of one of his relationships closely enough to know how things go down. From the outside, I've seen him go through a lot of women, but I never knew if he acted serious when he was with them. Did he tell them all he loved them? Is that just part of his game?

I don't want to believe that, but I feel so stupid for thinking I was special. I don't know what to think anymore.

I bring the food upstairs to my dad's place. He greets me like normal, and I do my best to act like I'm okay. He watches me set out our dinner with a furrow between his brows, so I know I'm not going to be able to hide anything from him. I have to tell him anyway, but I don't want to. He was the only other person in my life who knew, who saw Braxton and I together, acting like a couple. If I admit to him that it's over, I have to face the awful reality that it's true. Braxton used me, and left.

I try to make small talk, but it doesn't work very well, so I lapse into silence while we eat.

Dad slowly wipes his mouth with a napkin. "Are you going to tell me what's going on?"

I look down at my plate, my food hardly touched. I don't want to say it.

"Is this about Braxton?" he asks, his voice soft.

"Have you talked to him?" I ask.

"No," he says. "I haven't heard from him for several weeks. I've been wondering what's wrong."

He left my dad, too. Fucking hell. "Dad, he..." I'm not sure what to say. I can't even badmouth him. That's how fucked-up this breakup is. I should want to call him an asshole and tell my dad how much I hate him.

But I don't hate him at all.

I take a breath, hoping my burning eyes don't betray me. "He ended it."

"Oh, Kylie," Dad says. He reaches out and puts his twisted hand on top of mine.

Tears stream down my face. There's no stopping them.

"Sweetheart, I'm so sorry," he says.

I clamp my hand over my mouth and cry. I don't try to stop. Dad is blessedly quiet, letting me sob. I've cried a lot already, but here, with my dad's hand touching mine, the dam breaks. Hard.

"I'm sorry, Dad," I say, when I catch my breath. "I made such a mess of my life. I never should have fallen for him."

"I wish I understood what happened," he says. "Braxton loves you, Kylie. I don't know why he's doing this."

"No," I say, my voice emphatic. "No, he does not love me. Maybe in some weird Braxton world, he thought what he felt was love, but it wasn't. It wasn't real."

"I don't believe that," Dad says.

"Why are you taking his side?" I ask. "I didn't ask for this. He came home one night and that was it. He said it was a mistake—that we should have stayed friends, and he couldn't do it anymore. Do you know how much that hurt?"

"I'm not taking his side, sweetheart," Dad says. "But I know Braxton, better than he realizes. I'm crippled, but I'm not blind. I know how he is with women, but I also know he's loved you for years. He tried very hard to hide it, but I knew. He always looked at you the way I was afraid a man would look at you."

"Yeah, Dad, he looked at me like he wanted something from me," I say. "And sorry, I know I'm your daughter ... but let's just say he got it, and that was all he wanted."

"No," Dad says. "He looked at you like he loved you, even when you were both too young to know what that was."

I sniff and wipe the tears under my eyes. "Dad, Braxton doesn't know what love is."

"Oh, sweetheart. I'm sorry you're hurting."

"I know, Dad," I say. "I just have to figure out how to move on."

"Time," he says.

I look up and meet his eyes. We never talk about my mother, but I hear it in his voice. He knows exactly what I'm feeling right now.

"Time helps," he says. "It will get easier. And one day you'll realize you haven't thought about him for a while. Then it hurts again, because you feel bad about that. Eventually, even that starts to feel normal." He puts his hand on mine again. "I'm sorry, Kylie. I know how much he meant to you. Do you want me to call in any favors?"

I smile a little. "No."

He pats my hand. "Okay, sweetheart. You let me know if you change your mind."

We finish our meal, but it's not a very happy Thanksgiving. I clean up and kiss him goodbye. My heart feels so heavy, like it's taken up permanent residence in my feet, and a fresh wave of tears overtakes me as I drive home.

I flop down on the couch in my apartment, so emotionally exhausted I can't even cry anymore. The fact that it's the start of the holiday season only makes it worse. I think about my mother, and her new family. I bet they're all sitting around some huge table, laughing and eating and drinking expensive wine. I wonder if she thinks about me at all. Does she look at the people sitting around her table and feel like someone is missing? Does she ever think about sending me a Christmas card?

Probably not.

I'll have to spend Christmas with my dad, but other than that, I decide to skip the holidays this year. No presents, no decorations, no parties. I'm sure Selene will throw another New Year's Eve party, but there's no fucking way I'm going. I've completely avoided her since Braxton left me, and I don't know how I'm going to face her again. The loss of Selene cuts through me like another knife. I don't know what to do. Everything about her reminds me of Braxton; as much as I desperately want to lean on her right now, I can't.

I don't know if she and I can recover, and it's brutal as fuck because none of it is her fault.

It's not even nine, but I don't think I can handle life anymore today. I go to bed, wishing I could wake up in a world where the people I love don't abandon me.

26

BRAXTON

"Well, this is pretty much the worst Christmas in the history of ever." Selene looks at me with a bored expression, a glass of spiked eggnog in her hand. She decorated the house with a huge Christmas tree, lighted garlands, and some sort of candle that makes the whole place smell faintly like gingerbread.

"It isn't Christmas," I say.

"Well, it's supposed to be *our* Christmas. You're the one who had to be a pain in the ass and not come over on Christmas Day."

I don't give two shits about the holidays. I would have ignored the whole thing completely, but Selene insisted I come over.

I take a sip of the Scotch she bought me. It's smooth, goes down easy. I closed down the gym for the week, which is great news. It means I can get drunk and stay that way for a while.

"What did you expect?" I ask. "Fucking Christmas carolers?"

Selene scowls. "Why are you in such a mood?"

"I'm not in a mood," I say, although I'm not even trying to hide it from her anymore. I'm too fucking tired.

She gets up and takes her glass to the kitchen. "I don't know why I'm drinking this. It isn't even good. Can I have some of your Scotch?"

"Yeah, but bring it here and top me off."

I hear the bottle clink. "Fuck, Brax, we just opened it. Did you drink this much already?"

"Stop trying to be my mother."

She laughs. "Someone has to be."

She brings the bottle over and pours another splash. She tips the mouth away and I hold the glass up, raising my eyebrows at her until she pours more.

"Okay," she says, "I guess this is the kind of Christmas we're having this year." She takes the bottle back to the kitchen. "Have you talked to Kylie recently? What's she doing this week?"

Just hearing her name is a knife to my gut. I try not to flinch, although Selene can't see my face from where I'm sitting. "No, I haven't talked to her."

"Something is going on with her. I'm really worried."

I sit up. "Worried? Why?"

"Well, for one, she's hardcore avoiding me." She sits down on the other side of the sectional. "I've hardly seen her. It's so weird. I text her and she answers, but she cancels our plans every single time. I know she's busy with her design stuff, but it seems like it's more than that."

"I have no idea."

"When was the last time you guys hung out?" Selene asks.

I don't want to think about the last time I saw her—her cold and angry face, the edge of hatred in her voice. "Fuck, Selene, I don't know."

"Don't get all weird." She pauses, taking a sip of her Scotch. When she speaks again, her voice is different. Soft. Worried. "I think the guy she was seeing messed her up. I think he did something awful to her."

My chest clenches. "What?"

"I don't know for sure—she hasn't told me," she says. "But that's the thing. She won't tell me anything. He wasn't some guy she hooked up with a few times. It went on for months, as far as I can tell. But she kept the whole thing hidden, like there was something wrong. Think about it. There *was* something wrong. She was with someone she didn't want us to know about. I bet she knew we wouldn't approve of him. I think something really dark was going on, and she didn't want us to know about it."

I take a sip of my drink. I don't know what to say.

"Whoever he was, he must have done something awful to her," she says. "I think that's why she's avoiding me. She got hurt really bad, and she doesn't want to tell me."

Selene's eyes glisten with a hint of tears. I can feel her concern, her emotions leaking into me.

"I hope she's okay," I say, my voice soft. "But I honestly don't know."

She taps her fingernails against her glass, looking at me through narrowed eyes. "What is up with you lately?"

"Nothing." I need more Scotch.

"You say that like you can hide things from me," she says. "I know you. Something has been going on and you're not talking about it. God, between Kylie ignoring me and you being all broody and weird—" She stops talking midstream, her mouth hanging open. "Oh my god."

"What?"

Her dark eyes dig into me. "Braxton, did something happen between you and Kylie?"

Yes, I ruined us both. "No."

Her mouth opens wider, and she sets her drink on the coffee table. "Holy shit. You slept with her didn't you?"

I swallow hard, looking away. I can't lie again, so I don't say anything.

"Tell me," she says.

I stare at the floor.

"Tell me the goddamn truth," she says, her voice sharp. "You promised me, Braxton. You promised me you wouldn't do this. Did you lie to me?"

"Yes."

She sucks in a breath and I wince. The tirade is about to start. She stands up and paces around the living room. "For fuck's sake, Braxton. Really? Kylie? Do you see what you did?"

"I know what I did."

"No, you don't," she says. "You screwed us all over. Why couldn't you just keep it in your goddamn pants? You get every woman you want. Why did you have to add her to your list of fucking hookups?"

"It wasn't like that, Selene," I say. "I didn't hook up with her."

"You promised me you wouldn't," she says.

"It was too late."

She stops and puts her hands on her hips. "What? You had already slept with her?"

"Yes, but it wasn't—"

Selene cuts me off. "Goddamn it, Braxton, why did you do that? Why did you take my best friend from me?"

Anger pours through me, and I stand up, clenching my fists. "She was my best friend, too. I lost everything when I lost her." I'm breathing hard, and I want to put my fist through a wall.

Selene looks a little scared. "I knew this would happen," she says. "I knew if you fucked around with her you'd screw it up for all of us. Why did you have to use her like that?"

I'm so mad my vision is going blurry. I might have to leave before I break something. I'd never hurt Selene, not in a million years, but I don't want to scare her when I blow up. "I did *not* use her. I would *never*."

"This is what I was afraid of," Selene says, shouting at me. "I knew you would do this. You took her from me, damn it. Why did you fucking take her? She wasn't yours!"

My anger melts, emptiness spreading through my chest so fast I can't stop it. I fall back down to the couch and bury my face in my hands. My walls crumble.

She isn't mine.

Selene is silent for a long moment. I don't look up. I can't.

"Brax," she says, finally. Her tone is soft, with a hint of fear. "Brax, what's going on? What are you doing?" I feel her sit down next to me. "What aren't you telling me?"

"I loved her," I say. I can barely choke out the words. My eyes burn. I have to get my shit together. I've never cried in front of anyone in my life—especially not my sister.

"What?" Selene breathes.

I take a deep breath and find my voice, my face still in my hands. "I loved her, Selene. I've always loved her. When she broke up with Derek, I told her."

"That was months ago," she says.

I nod.

"So, you were..." She pauses. "There wasn't some dumb guy with a big dick. She was with you that whole time?"

"Yeah, she was with me," I say. Now that I've admitted the truth, I can't seem to stop. "It was everything, Selene. She was everything. I've loved her for as long as I can remember, and I finally had her. She was mine, and we were so good together. I wanted to tell you. I was such an idiot for lying. We wanted to wait until the time was right, because we knew you'd be upset. But the right time never seemed to come, and I kept lying. Fuck, that was a stupid thing to do. I'm sorry we lied to you. I should have told you from the beginning."

"Wait." She leans away from me. "You're saying you guys were actually together. Like, in a relationship, together?"

"Yeah."

"Not just sleeping together?"

"Yes." I sit back and lean my head against the cushions. "It was so much more than that."

"But you guys broke up?" she asks. "I'm so confused."

My head fucking hurts. I pinch the bridge of my nose. "I promised you."

"Promised me?" Selene asks. She gasps, putting a hand to her mouth. "Oh my god. When I talked to you that day, you were already with her ... and you thought you had to break up with her for me?"

I don't understand why she sounds so panicked. It's not like she's the one who got her heart smashed to pieces. "What the fuck was I supposed to do?" I ask. "You made it clear that you couldn't live with Kylie and I being together. You're my sister. How was I supposed to choose between you?"

Selene puts her hand on my shoulder. "Oh, Brax. I'm so sorry. I didn't know. I never would have said that if I knew."

I stare at her. "What the fuck are you talking about?"

"I was always afraid you'd hook up with Kylie, like all those other girls," she says. "You'd have sex a few times, and get bored or whatever it is you do. She wouldn't be able to go on being friends with you after that. What was I supposed to think? You don't exactly have a history of commitment."

I look away, my gut churning. I thought I was getting better, but this conversation is making me feel worse all over again. "Look, you don't want us together, that's fine. I'll do what I have to do. And Kylie will come around. She'll get over me, and the two of you will be good again. I'll stay out of the way so you can still be her friend." I stand up and go to the kitchen. My glass isn't empty, but I want more anyway.

"No," she says.

"No?" I ask. "What more do you want from me, Selene? I gave up everything for you."

Tears leak out of the corners of her eyes, trailing down her cheeks.

"Why are you crying?" I ask.

"This is my fault," she says.

"No, it isn't."

She sniffs. "Okay, it's mostly your fault, because you lied. But it's a little bit my fault. I didn't want to hurt you like this. Do you really think I'm that selfish? That I'd make you leave her?"

I put my glass down on the counter. "It's not about being selfish. Kylie is important to you. You needed things to stay the same. Of course, I screwed that up, too. I never should have told Kylie I loved her. I should have just kept pretending I didn't."

"You really love her?" Selene asks.

"Yeah, I do, Selene. I always have. But it doesn't matter anymore."

"Of course it matters. Braxton, what are we talking about here? Love? Like, the real kind?"

"Yes, the real kind." I don't want to talk about this.

"The forever kind?" she asks.

"I would have loved her forever. I would have married her."

Selene's mouth drops open. "What did you just say?"

I take a big gulp of Scotch. Holy shit, I just said it, didn't I? I've never said it out loud. But I mean it. I put the glass down. "I would have married her, Selene. In a heartbeat."

"This is huge." Selene slowly stands up from the couch. "This is the biggest thing that's ever happened to us."

I shake my head. "No, it isn't, because no one is marrying anyone. I broke her heart, remember? I did exactly what I promised her I wouldn't do."

"So?"

"So, she hates me," I say. "She told me she never wants to see me again. And trust me, she meant it."

"What are you going to do?" she asks.

"Do? I'm going to drink Scotch until I'm numb. I'm going to stay as shit-faced as possible until I have to go back to work, and then I'm going to try to survive this. Even though I don't particularly want to."

"You aren't going to fight for her?" she asks.

"There's nothing left to fight for," I say. "I broke us both."

"Then put the two of you back together," Selene says. She walks over to the other side of the counter. "We need a plan."

"You're drunk."

"I'm not drunk," she says. "And you aren't getting drunk either. We're going to get Kylie back."

"We?"

"Yes, *we*," she says. "You did this because of me, and she won't see me either, so we both have apologies to make. But we are going to fix this, Braxton."

I stare at Selene. "You want me to try to get her back?"

"Of course I do," Selene says. "I want you to be happy.

Honestly, Braxton, I've always known you had thing for Kylie, but I figured you just wanted to bang her. But if you love her, you should be with her. That's kind of amazing."

A tiny shred of hope worms its way into my mind. Is it possible? Kylie said she never wanted to see me again, but that was because I pushed her away. Do I still have a chance?

I clutch my chest like I need to restart my heart. Fuck, I miss her so much.

I look up at Selene. "Okay, what do we do?"

27

KYLIE

I take a deep breath to settle the flutter of nerves as I wait for my flight. I look up at the screen. *Seattle to London, departing 3:15, on time.* I check the time on my phone. I have about ten minutes before they'll start boarding.

Braxton and I were supposed to go to London for New Year's. He even bought tickets. When he left me, I didn't even think about this trip—but a couple of weeks ago I decided to go. I've wanted to spend New Year's Eve in London for years, and I keep putting it off. This year I have extra money from my design clients, so I decided to splurge. I don't know what happened to the tickets Braxton bought; I'm sure he canceled them. I bought my own, booked a hotel, and now I'm really doing it.

I bring up my dad's number and hit send.

"Hey, Kylie," Dad says. "Are you at the airport?"

"Yeah, I'm waiting to board."

"I want you to have a great time, all right?"

"I will."

"Be safe," he says. "I don't know how I feel about you traveling so far by yourself."

"Dad, I'll be fine," I say. "I'll be home in a few days."

"That's a long way to go for such a short trip," he says.

"I know, but I need to get back for work," I say. "And, I don't know, I have a feeling it's going to be worth it."

"It will be," he says. "Call me when you land."

I smile. "I will. Love you, Dad."

"Love you too, sweetheart."

I hang up, and the announcement for first class boarding blares through the speakers. First class would be great—it's a long flight—but my splurging didn't go that far.

I wait for my turn to board, fiddling with the zipper on my purse. I have my whole trip planned out. I'm going to museums, the theater, shopping. I fly home on New Year's Day, so my last night I'm going to fulfill my silly bucket list item and watch Big Ben tick over to midnight. From what I saw online, there's a pretty spectacular fireworks show.

I board the plane and take my seat, stowing my purse near my feet, then get out my phone and plug in headphones. I have my new *let's have an adventure* playlist all queued up. I tuck a few magazines into the pocket in front of me and sit back, getting as comfortable as I can. I'm going to be here a while.

I glance at my phone, wondering if I should text Selene. I haven't seen her in weeks, and I made some excuse about not being around for Christmas. She'll be pretty weirded out to find out I left for London without letting her know. But I can't bring myself to do it. I miss her, but I know nothing will ever be the same between us. There's such a huge gulf now, and I don't know if I can bridge it.

The worst part is, it's as much my fault as Braxton's. I lied to her, too.

I lean my head back and close my eyes. I don't want to think about Braxton, but that's essentially impossible. He left a hole inside me that no one will ever fill. I miss him so much it hurts, a deep ache that I don't think will ever go away. Not completely.

I wait while the plane fills, and it isn't long before we're taxiing down the runway. I look down at my phone again. He's not going to call. It's been six weeks, and I haven't heard a word from him.

I turn my phone to airplane mode and close my eyes, relaxing as the plane takes off.

28

BRAXTON

"It's going straight to voicemail," Selene says. "Should I leave a message?"

"No," I say. "Not yet. Maybe her phone is dead. She always forgets to plug it in."

Selene puts her phone down on the counter. So far, our thirty minutes of planning over Scotch has gotten us as far as Selene calling Kylie, since we both know she won't pick up for me.

After that? I have no fucking clue.

"Should we go over to her apartment?" Selene asks.

I'm buzzing too hard to get behind the wheel. "Can you drive?"

"Good point," she says. She moves the Scotch out of reach. "We could Uber, but we need to sober up anyway." She pours us a couple glasses of ice water. "I can text her, and when she charges her phone, she'll answer. At least then we'll know we can call."

"Okay," I say. "That's a start."

She types out a text. "There. Now I guess we wait?"

I blow out a breath. This sucks. I'm so amped, I can barely stand still. I walk from the kitchen to the living room so I can pace. "I hate waiting."

"You have to figure out what you're going to say to her."

I pause and glance over my shoulder. "You're not helping."

"I'm serious," Selene says.

"I'll figure it out when I see her," I say.

"Tell you what," Selene says. "Stay here tonight. Who knows when she'll answer. As soon as she does, we'll ... do whatever it is we're going to do. But in the meantime, let's watch a movie or something so you don't wear a hole in my new rug."

I take a deep breath and rub my hands over my face again. I don't think I'll be able to relax until I see Kylie, but there's not much I can do about it right now.

I ROLL over and almost fall off the couch. Fuck, I fell asleep out here. I should have gone to bed, but I didn't think I was ever going to drift off.

I get up and run a hand through my hair. I don't see any sign of Selene, but her phone is on the coffee table. Her message notification blinks. I swipe my thumb across the screen, but she has a fucking passcode. Damn it.

I haul ass up the stairs and knock on her door. "Selene. What's the passcode on your phone?"

I hear a muffled reply through the door.

"Selene, get up. You have a message."

She comes to the door, tying a belted robe around her waist. Her hair is a mess, and she rubs her eyes. She grabs the phone and makes a little triangle across the screen with her thumb.

"Is it Kylie?" I ask.

"Yeah," Selene says. Her brow furrows. "All it says is, 'Sorry I missed your text. Been busy. Catch up soon.' But it's timestamped at 3:27 am. Why was she texting me back at three twenty-seven?"

Busy? At three in the morning? What was she doing?

Fuck, was she with someone?

"Call her," I say.

"Braxton, it's six o'clock in the morning. If she was up a few hours ago, she's probably—"

"Just call."

Selene stifles a yawn behind her hand and calls. She puts the phone to her ear but shakes her head. "Voicemail."

"Did it ring?"

"Nope," she says. "I bet her phone is off."

"Fuck."

"Come on, Brax, it's early. Go back to bed for a few hours. We'll call her later."

I head to my room, but I know I won't be able to sleep. Instead, I shower and put on clean clothes. Selene is still in her room when I come out, so I quietly leave through the front door.

I drive by Kylie's place, and see her car. I almost go up to her door, but I decide to wait—partly because there's something I want to do first, and partly because I'm half-terrified she's not alone.

"WHERE WERE YOU?" Selene asks when I walk in the door a few hours later.

"I had to take care of something," I say. "I drove by Ky's. Her car was there."

"Did you see her?" Selene asks, her voice excited.

"No, it was still early," I say. "And fuck, Selene, what if she was with someone last night?"

A flicker of pain crosses Selene's face. "I know, I thought of that, too. But she probably wasn't. Let's not get all freaked out until we know what's going on."

"Has she called?"

"No," Selene says. "And I tried again a couple times. Straight to voicemail. She's going to think I'm a psycho when she checks her missed calls."

"Let's just go to her place. If she's got someone there..." I can't even think it. "I don't know, but I can't sit around waiting for her to turn on her phone."

We pull up outside Kylie's place. Her car is still there, parked in her usual spot. My heart thunders as we walk up to her door. Selene and I both have keys, but I knock.

Nothing.

Selene looks worried. She pulls out her phone and checks it again, as if she's hoping we might magically have a message from Kylie.

I knock again. We wait.

No answer.

"What the fuck?" I ask.

"I hate to say this, but maybe she didn't sleep here last night," Selene says.

My gut twists. I know Selene is right. If she was out with someone, he could have picked her up, which is why her car is still here. And if things went well, she might have gone home with him.

"Let's check inside," I say, and pull out my keys.

"What? No, we can't go in."

"Why not?" I ask.

"This is basically breaking and entering, you realize that, right?"

"I have a key."

"This is a bad idea," Selene says. But she still follows me inside.

Kylie definitely isn't here. Everything is spotless. No dishes in the sink, no random crap left out on the couch or coffee table. I glance in her bedroom. The bed is made and there's no sign she's been here recently.

It doesn't look like she slept at home last night.

My chest feels hollow again, the emptiness taking over. I'm too late.

"I'm sorry." Selene rubs her hand across my back. "Would she have stayed over at her dad's?"

"No," I say. "She never sleeps there."

Selene sighs and looks around. Her phone buzzes in her hand and she almost drops it. She puts a hand to her mouth and looks.

My heart races again. "Is it her?"

"Yeah," Selene says. She looks up and meets my eyes. "She says she's in London."

I burst out laughing.

"What?" Selene asks. "Why the fuck is that funny? What's she doing in London?"

Holy shit, I'm so proud of her. "It's something she's always wanted to do. We were supposed to go for New Year's. I returned the tickets already, but I guess she decided to go. Quick, ask her if she's alone."

Selene types and we wait.

"She says she went by herself."

Elation pours through me and I put a hand on my chest. She's not with someone else. I can still do this. "Oh, fuck. That's the best thing I've heard in six weeks. Let's go."

I head for the front door.

"Where are we going now?" Selene asks.

"Home to pack," I say. "We're going to London."

29

BRAXTON

Getting a flight on such short notice proves to be a challenge. The next five flights with seats left all have layovers in places like Chicago and Denver—cities currently blanketed in snow. There's no way I'm going to risk getting stuck in a fucking blizzard before I can get to London. I want to leave sooner, but I book a nonstop flight that leaves tomorrow, and has us landing in London at noon on New Year's Eve.

Waiting feels like an eternity. I insist on getting to the airport three hours early. Selene is annoyed, but I'd rather sit at the gate than risk getting caught in security and missing the flight.

I sip a cup of coffee while Selene lounges with a book next to me. The airport is busy, people coming and going all around us.

"I hate to say this now," Selene says, "but you know we could wait until she comes home, right? It's not like she moved. She's just on a little vacation."

I shake my head. "No."

"I mean, we're here, and we're going," she says. "I just needed to point out that this is kind of crazy."

"If we could have flown out yesterday, I would have," I say. "I'm not waiting a minute longer than I have to."

Selene smiles at me.

"What?" I ask.

"Nothing." She shakes her head. "I just never thought I'd see the day."

"What day?"

"Never mind."

Our flight is delayed. Of course it is. We wait another two hours before we finally board. Once we're on, I can hardly sit still; Selene keeps smacking my knee to make me stop fidgeting.

Ten hours is a long time to be cooped up in a giant metal tube that's hurtling through the air at thirty thousand feet. I have a drink to calm down, and eventually I doze for a while. Selene sleeps for a few hours with her head on my arm.

By the time we touch down, I'm wide awake again. The landing gear hits the runway, and I'm buzzing with adrenaline. I have no idea where Kylie is, or how I'm going to find her. Selene checks her messages when we have cell service again, and Kylie hasn't replied to any of her texts. I hope she's checking in with her dad regularly, because this dead phone thing when she's in a foreign country is bullshit.

We didn't check bags, but it takes a little while to get through customs and immigration. When we get out of the airport, Selene calls Kylie's dad to see if he knows where she is. I would call him, but I'm not sure how he feels about me. He must know what I did to Kylie, and I owe him an apology, but right now, we're in a city of almost nine million people and all I can think about is finding her.

"Hi, Henry," Selene says when he answers. "Yeah, I'm good. Listen, I'm going to cut to the chase. Do you know where Kylie is? Right, I know she's in London. Do you know where in London?" Selene waits for a moment, listening. "Yeah, we've been trying to call her too." Selene meets my eyes. "Oh, her battery was dying and she needed to get an adapter so she could plug it in? Okay, but where is she staying? Um, we're actually here. Yes, in London. Yeah, I'm with Braxton. Exactly. We literally just landed. Okay, Morton Hotel. Got it. Yes, I'll call you later."

She hangs up. "Morton Hotel."

I'm already looking it up on my phone. We get in line for a taxi. The tube would be cheaper, but I don't give a fuck at this point.

The taxi drops us off in front of the hotel. The entry is nice, with a tall arched doorway, glass doors, and stone accents. I head straight for the front desk. I know they won't tell me what room Kylie's in, but I figure I can get Selene a room for the night so we have a place to put our stuff. We didn't bring much, but there's no sense in carrying it all over the city if we have to go out and search for her.

I don't bother getting a room for myself. I plan to be with Kylie tonight.

"Can I leave a message for another guest?" I ask, when I have Selene's room taken care of.

"Of course," the front desk attendant says. "Room number?"

"I'm actually not sure," I say. "I don't suppose you could look it up and tell me?"

"I'm afraid not," she says.

I shake my head. "Of course not." I grab one of the business cards and scrawl a note on the back.

I love you. Brax

"Can you just make sure this gets to Kylie Winters' room?"

"Yes, that won't be a problem," she says.

"Thanks."

I hand Selene her room key and we head for the stairs.

"What do we do now?" she asks.

"You look exhausted, so why don't you go lie down," I say. "I'll wait down here for a while and see if she comes through the lobby."

"God, Braxton, she could be anywhere," Selene says.

"I know. We'll find her."

She takes a deep breath. "Okay, call me if you see her."

"I will."

Selene takes my backpack and goes upstairs. I find a chair that gives me a good view of the lobby and front entrance. I'm tired as shit, but I don't want to miss her if she walks by.

I WAKE UP WITH A START. Fuck, I fell asleep in the damn lobby. I check my phone, but I don't have any calls or texts. It's five-thirty. I must have been out for about an hour. I hope I didn't miss her. I guess there's not much chance that she would walk by and not see me—except that she's not expecting me to be here. I hope the front desk got my note to her room. She'll see it's my handwriting. She'll have to know I'm here.

I should probably stay in one place and wait for her to come to me, but after ten minutes, I can't stand it anymore. It's stupid to think I can wander around this huge city and actually find her—but fuck it, I need to do something, not just sit on my ass. I consider waking Selene so she can come do lobby duty, but I decide to let her sleep. She'd probably just fall asleep in the chair like I did. An overnight flight and an eight-hour time difference are no joke.

Walking aimlessly through London isn't going to cut it, so I think about what I know. Where would Kylie go? What would she want to see? I pull up some travel info on my phone, pick a few places that sound right, and head out into the cold.

The sun is already down; the clear sky is going to make for a freezing night. I have a coat, but I pop into a shop and buy a dark gray hat and scarf, and a pair of black leather gloves. I've been to London once before, and navigating around the city comes back to me pretty quickly. I take the tube, coming up at various places where I think I might find her. I check my phone way too often, hoping she'll get my note and call.

I try to ignore the fact that she could easily get my note and *not* call.

I stop in another shop and buy her an adapter so she can charge her fucking phone.

By nine, I'm starving, so I grab some food and take it back to the hotel. Selene is up and showered. She asks how my evening went, but I don't have anything to show for it except sore feet.

"So, what should we do?" Selene asks after we finish eating. "Watch for her in the lobby?"

I check the time. It's just after ten. Still no call.

"How about you hang out downstairs and keep watch," I say. "I can't sit down there doing nothing. I'll go nuts. I have a couple more ideas."

"Okay, if that's what you think is best."

I leave Selene in the lobby and head out into the cold. I pass a few pubs with New Year's Eve parties starting up, but

I don't see Kylie. I keep telling myself my instincts are going to lead me to her, but I strike out everywhere I go.

I take the tube again to a different part of the city. I find a place that serves coffee and warm up for a little while. Even all bundled up, I'm fucking freezing. Selene texts me once to check in, but she hasn't seen her. There's a party going on in the hotel bar, and Selene reports doing a couple laps through the crowd to see if Kylie is there, but so far, no luck.

I'm starting to think Selene was right. We should have just waited until she came home. Mr. Winters said she's flying home tomorrow anyway. It would have been a hell of a lot easier—and cheaper—to just wait. Maybe I am crazy.

But I couldn't wait. I still can't. The clock is ticking toward midnight, and I'm overcome with a deep sense of urgency. If I let her start the new year without me, I'm afraid I'll end it without her. Afraid my chance will be gone.

I think about where we were a year ago. I remember her at my sister's party—standing in the kitchen, dressed in that hot little black dress and sexy red heels, ditched by whatever jackass Selene set her up with. I almost kissed her, right then. I was probably drunk, and it would have been a stupid thing to do. I was dating someone else at the time. I knew she'd been counting on starting her year off right. We'd talked the day before about resolutions and making changes. In the back of my mind, the thought bloomed: What if this was our year? What if next New Year's Eve I was the one kissing her?

I almost had it. And now my chance is ticking away with every minute.

That's when it hits me.

Big Ben. She wanted to watch it hit midnight.

I rush out of the restaurant to the nearest tube station.

Fuck, how do I get there? I look at the map, figuring out the route, and board the right train.

I check the time. Eleven forty-two. Shit. How long is this going to take?

The train stops. I dash out and run up to the street.

Half of fucking London is here. The crowd is huge, the cold obviously not keeping people from coming out to celebrate. I'm inundated by crazy hats, waving glow sticks, necklaces with blinking lights. I push my way into the mass, keeping the huge clock in my sights.

I'm never going to find her in this.

I make my way closer to Westminster, but the crowd gets thicker. I know she's out here somewhere. She has to be. It's why she came. I glance up at the clock. Five minutes.

My phone vibrates, but it's a text from Selene. *Any luck?*

I type a quick *no* and keep looking.

My breath comes out in a cloud in the cold air. I look into the faces of everyone I pass, desperate.

Fuck, Kylie, I'm here. I came all this way. Where are you?

Eleven fifty-six.

People are packed around me. She isn't here. She hates big crowds. She wouldn't stand here; she'd be where she can see without suffocating. I turn around and start pushing my way back toward the edge of the crowd. I check my phone again.

Eleven fifty-seven.

The energy around me rises, people cheering, blowing noisemakers, holding up cell phones to take pictures. Some drunk asshole stumbles into me, and I catch him, pushing him back to his feet while he laughs. I get to where the crowd thins out and stop, looking around.

Eleven fifty-eight.

I see her before she sees me. My chest tightens; the

breath rushes from my lungs. God, she's beautiful. She's bundled up in a cream-colored hat and a black coat with a thick collar. Her cheeks are flushed from the cold, and she's staring at the clock, blowing into her hands to warm them.

My heart tries to break free from my ribs. I'm overcome —desperate to hold her again, terrified she won't forgive me. I force myself to walk toward her, focusing on each step.

Her face turns and her eyes widen. Her lips part in surprise.

She sees me.

30

KYLIE

I stare at the man walking toward me, my heart suddenly racing. It can't be Braxton. I'm in London. He doesn't know where I am. And even if he found out, he's in Seattle. He's not here.

Except he is.

He's as gorgeous as ever, goddamn him. He's wearing a dark wool coat and scarf, and he pulls off a pair of black leather gloves, tucking them in his pocket. A hat covers his hair, but it only emphasizes his rugged jaw and smoldering brown eyes.

My belly flip-flops and my heart beats too fast. I'm completely frozen, staring in disbelief. I can't decide if I want to collapse into his arms and cry, or slap him for showing up here and ruining my New Year's Eve.

I want to be angry. I want to turn my back and tell him I meant it when I said I never wanted to see him again. But he moves closer, and his expression unmakes me. A groove forms between his eyes and the lines of his jaw stand out. He looks so … wounded. His eyes move over me like he never expected to see me again.

Maybe he didn't.

The crowd starts to count down.

Ten ... nine ...

He stands right in front of me, his eyes full of so much pain. Mine fill with tears, and I bite my lip to keep them from spilling over.

Eight ... seven ...

He doesn't look away, holding my gaze with his. I'm transfixed. His presence is mesmerizing.

Six ... five ...

I tilt my face up as he moves in closer.

Four ... three ...

He leans down. I can see how hard he's breathing.

Two ...

His hand slips into my open coat, around my waist, and he draws me close.

One.

He claims my mouth with his, pushing his tongue in deep. I open for him, sucking in a hard breath, and grab his coat. I pull him closer. His lips on mine feel so good, so perfect, so right. Oh god, I missed him so much. A tear leaks from the corner of my eye, running down my cheek. His arms wrap around me, strong and possessive. He holds the back of my head, keeping our mouths locked together. I couldn't pull away if I tried.

I cling to the lapels of his coat, falling, crashing, crumbling to pieces. I'm consumed by him—taken. Vaguely, I hear the fireworks, the huge crowd cheering.

He doesn't stop kissing me. I'm surrounded by his scent, intoxicating and familiar. His mouth, so warm and soft. I melt against him, my body going fluid. I'm surprised my legs will still hold me up.

He pulls back, but our lips don't part. He holds me there, his breath hot on my face, his arms around me.

My shoulders shake, and the tears come.

He breaks the kiss and holds me against him while I sob into his chest. It can't be him. This can't be real.

He speaks softly, his mouth next to my ear. "Kylie, I am so sorry. Please tell me I didn't lose you forever. Please, baby girl." His voice breaks. "I love you."

I lean back so I can look up at him, tears still running down my face. He wipes my cheek with his thumb. My throat feels thick and I'm not sure I can get any words out. I open my mouth, my lower lip still trembling. "I love you, too."

His legs buckle slightly, and he grabs onto me. For a second I think we both might fall over, but he's steady. He clings to me, burying his face in my neck. "Oh, god, Kylie, I fucking love you so much," he says, speaking low into my ear. "I'll never leave you again. I swear. Never."

I tremble against him, trying to catch my breath. I wrap my arms around his neck and hold onto him for dear life.

Braxton. My Braxton.

After long moments, he pulls away. The loud bang of fireworks continues, the crowd cheering with every explosion.

I finally find my voice again. "What are you doing here?"

"I had to come see you," he says. "I couldn't wait."

Reality coalesces in my mind, the truth of what I'm seeing: Braxton, standing here, in London, in the middle of the night.

"How long have you been here?"

"We got in earlier today," he says. "We've been trying to find you for hours."

"We?"

"Yeah, Selene's watching the hotel lobby in case you come back."

I gape at him, astounded. "Selene's here?"

He nods. "Of course she is. She wanted to help."

"Help? I don't understand."

"Kylie, I made such a mistake. Leaving you was the stupidest fucking thing I've ever done, and I've done a lot of stupid things in my life." He puts a hand on my cheek. "I didn't mean a word I said that night. I thought I had to do it. I thought I had to choose between you and my sister, and I didn't know what else to do. But I was wrong. I was so wrong, and I'll do anything to make it right."

I take a breath, my body shivering. "I can't believe you're here."

"It took me too long to figure out where you'd be," he says. "I almost didn't make it."

"Braxton, you flew halfway across the world for this?"

"Yeah," he says, and the groove forms between his eyes again, his expression intensifying. "I did. I had to. I have something to ask you, and it couldn't wait. It had to be tonight."

He touches my face, his eyes sweeping over me like they did the first night he told me he wanted me. The night everything changed.

My breath quickens again.

"Kylie," he says, his voice gravelly. Before I know what's happening, he takes my hands in his and sinks down onto one knee.

My eyes widen and my mouth drops open, my breath catching in my throat. He can't be—

"I love you, baby girl. Always have. I'm yours, and I want you to be mine, forever." He reaches into his inside pocket and pulls something out, pinched between his thumb and two fingers.

A ring.

I clamp my hand over my mouth.

He smiles—that brain-melting smile that makes me forget where I am, that sucks all the oxygen from the air. "What do you say, Ky? Will you marry me?"

I meet his eyes. He's so open, so honest. Holding nothing back.

My eyes tear up again, but it's laughter that escapes my lips.

"Yes," I say, though I can hardly get the word out. I'm smiling and laughing and crying all at once.

He stands, wrapping his arms around me, and lifts me off my feet. My face is even with his, and he kisses me, his lips like silk. People around us clap and cheer, and I'm pretty sure I see the flash of a few cameras. He sets me down and takes my left hand. He meets my eyes while he slips the ring on my finger.

"There," he says, his voice soft. "Now you're mine forever."

EPILOGUE: KYLIE

Selene plucks the glass of champagne from my hand. "You can't get drunk before your wedding."

I laugh. "I'm not getting drunk. I've had one glass."

She smiles and goes back to putting on my eyeliner. "Well, you're making it hard for me to do your makeup."

I hold still, looking down while she smudges the eyeliner with her finger. I haven't put on my dress yet, but my hair is done, falling in loose waves around my shoulders. I didn't want anything too formal but the hairstylist was amazing. I don't think I've ever felt so beautiful.

Selene puts a coat of mascara on my eyelashes, then stops, inspecting her handiwork. She brushes something from beneath my eyes. "There. You look..." She trails off, and her expression changes. Her brow creases; her eyes fill with tears.

"Stop it," I say, smacking her on the arm. "You have to quit crying or I'm going to mess up my makeup."

She puts her hand to her mouth. "I'm sorry, Kylie, I just can't help it. You look so beautiful, and you're marrying my brother, and that means…"

I pull her in for a hug. "We've always been sisters, babe," I say quietly into her ear.

"I love you."

I bite my lip so I won't cry. "I love you, too."

Selene takes a deep breath. "Okay, sorry. I'll stop. Let's get you dressed."

She helps me into my gown. It's strapless and sleek, with just enough beading on the bodice to give it a little sparkle. I move my hair aside so Selene can zip it up the back.

Ellen, the wedding coordinator, pokes her head in through the door. "Almost ready?"

"Yeah," I say.

Selene smiles at me again. She looks fabulous in a silver off-the-shoulder floor-length gown. Her dark hair is pinned up, with a few loose tendrils hanging down.

"Great, we're just waiting on the groom," Ellen says and closes the door.

I look at Selene in alarm. "Waiting on the groom? He's not here?"

"Don't panic," Selene says with a laugh. "He probably just left his tie at home or something."

I was already nervous, but a renewed tingle of fear runs through me. There's no way Braxton wouldn't show. I saw him yesterday for the rehearsal, and he didn't even seem nervous.

"He should have been here an hour ago," I say.

"I'll text him," Selene says and picks up her phone.

I chew on my lower lip and look away.

"Ky," Selene says. "You can't be worried he isn't coming. He's more excited about this than anyone—maybe even you."

She's absolutely right. I tried to talk Braxton into waiting until next New Year's Eve to get married—because how romantic would that be?—but he wouldn't even consider it. He wanted the earliest date possible. If it wasn't for my dad, he probably would have taken me to a courthouse as soon as we got back from London. But we both knew my dad wanted to be a part of this. So we planned an April wedding, throwing it together on short notice. It wasn't too hard. Neither of us have much family; it's mostly just the three of us and my dad. We invited some friends, but it's going to be small and intimate.

"I know," I say. "But what if something happened to him?"

"He's a guy," Selene says. "He probably figured he could leave ten minutes before the wedding started and now he's stuck in traffic."

Ellen opens the door again. "Kylie, can you come out and take a few pictures with your dad? He's out here waiting for you."

I take a deep breath, trying to relax, and grab my bouquet. Selene and I come out of the small room we were using to get ready. We were lucky enough to book a classy little boutique hotel in downtown Seattle. The guests are already seated one of the smaller banquet rooms where we're having both the ceremony and a cocktail reception.

I see my dad waiting in the hallway. He turns his chair around and his face breaks into a wide smile.

He takes my hand. "Kylie, you look beautiful."

"Thanks," I say, and swallow hard to keep from tearing up again. He's dressed in a gray suit with a silver tie. "You look great, too." Even seated in his chair, he looks so handsome.

The photographer takes a few pictures of the two of us. I notice Ellen lingering near the entrance to the banquet room where our guests are waiting. She looks at her watch repeatedly.

Fuck, where is he?

I turn to Selene. "Has he texted yet?"

"Crap," she says. "I left my phone in the other room."

"Who are you looking for?" Dad asks.

"Braxton," I say. "He's not here yet."

Dad shakes his head. "Oh, no, he—"

"Did someone order a groom?"

I turn to find Braxton walking toward us, a sly smile on his face.

I almost drop my flowers. He looks exquisite in a slate gray suit and silver tie, his stubble trimmed perfectly. I don't think the day will ever come when that man doesn't take my breath away. He's gorgeous.

His eyes come to rest on me, and he stops in his tracks, putting a hand to his chest. "Holy shit, Kylie. You're stunning."

"Brax," Selene says with a laugh, "you're not supposed to see her yet. It's the rules."

"I don't like rules," he says. He comes toward me, his eyes never leaving mine, and leans down to kiss me lightly on the lips.

"You're late," I say.

"I know." He kisses my nose.

I laugh. "You need to get in there. Our wedding is about to start."

He glances at my dad. "Actually," he says, "there's a slight change of plans."

"What do you mean?"

"Are we ready?" Ellen asks, her voice bright. "Come on, over here, everyone." She ushers us toward the double doors that lead to the banquet room, and gestures for Selene to stand in front.

"Wait, we can't start yet," I say. "Braxton, you're supposed to be in there. We rehearsed this."

Ellen opens the doors and Selene walks in.

Braxton produces a silver cane and hands it to my dad. "Like I said, change of plans. You ready for this, Mr. Winters?"

My dad takes the cane and plants it on the floor. Braxton takes his arm and helps him stand.

My mouth drops open. "Dad."

"Are you steady?" Braxton asks.

My dad straightens his back, standing tall. My eyes fill with tears. I haven't seen my dad stand in over a year.

"Dad, how did you do that?"

He smiles. "I've been working with Braxton on my strength. I wanted to be able to walk my little girl down the aisle." He holds his arm out for me.

"Oh, Dad." I take a shuddering breath and tuck my hand in the crook of his elbow.

Braxton puts his hand on my arm. "Sorry I was late, baby girl. I had to go get his cane. I need to walk in with you in case he needs help. Is that okay?"

"Of course it's okay," I say, trying very hard not to let more tears spill down my cheeks.

Ellen gestures again, and the three of us start down the aisle. I keep my hand on my dad's arm, and he leans on his cane. Braxton walks on his other side.

I'm so overwhelmed, I'm not sure how I make it up the aisle.

When we reach the front, Dad turns to me. He has tears in his eyes and all hope of not ruining my makeup is gone. "I love you, sweetheart."

"I love you too, Dad." I hug him, careful not to make him lose his balance.

Braxton keeps him steady with a hand on his arm. Dad pulls away. Braxton still has his hand on Dad's arm, and Dad places his hand over the top of Braxton's. "Thank you, son."

Braxton's eyes glisten. He blows out a breath and smiles, wrapping my dad in a gentle hug. Dad's nurse has his chair ready for him, and he takes careful steps to the side and sits down.

I hand my flowers to Selene, and Braxton stands in front of me. He takes my hands, his eyes never leaving mine. I'm vaguely aware of the officiant speaking, and I know there's a small group of people watching from their seats, but it all falls away. Braxton is everything.

Our vows are simple, and I say mine first, looking up into his eyes. When it's Braxton's turn, he shifts closer, his face tilted toward mine. His words are only for me.

"I, Braxton Taylor, take you, Kylie Winters to be my wife. I promise to love you, honor you, and cherish you from this day forward." He places one hand alongside my face, swiping away a tear with his thumb. "I love you, Ky. I always have. I want nothing more than to be yours for the rest of my life."

I take a trembling breath and smile up at him.

I hear the officiant say the words—"By the power vested in me by the state of Washington, I now pronounce you man and wife."—but I don't see anything but Braxton.

I think he's supposed to say *you may kiss the bride*, but Braxton doesn't wait.

He slips his hand around to the back of my head, threading his fingers through my hair, and brings his mouth to mine. He holds nothing back, kissing me with all the passion I've ever felt from him. His tongue caresses mine with tenderness, lighting me up inside. I melt into him, feeling his strength, his warmth. He's always been my rock, my safety, my soft place to land. His hands are steady and strong, his lips so soft against mine.

He pulls away and hesitates, his nose brushing against mine. My eyes flutter open, and he smiles. Our little crowd of guests clap, and I think we're supposed to walk back down the aisle now, but he surges in again, kissing me hard. I wrap my arms around his neck and he lifts me up off my feet, holding me tight against him. I'm so light, I could almost fly.

He's here. He's real. He's everything.

Always.

AFTERWORD

Dear reader,

Sometimes a story comes out of nowhere and knocks me upside the head and won't leave me alone until I write it. It doesn't happen very often, but when it does, it's creative gold.

ALWAYS HAVE was that story. There were times when I'd wake up in the middle of the night with words knocking around in my brain, and I'd have to get up and write so I could go back to sleep. I remember wandering through the grocery store one day, my head so full of these characters, it took me twice as long to get my shopping done because I had such a hard time focusing on reality.

Okay, the *not focused on reality* part is kind of me all the time. But when I was writing this book, it was really bad.

Braxton and Kylie became so real to me. That generally happens with my characters—the heroes and heroines from my Jetty Beach series feel very real. But Brax and Ky took that up a notch. I'm not sure why. I FELT them, deep in my bones, in my soul.

That's made releasing this book to the public a strangely

emotional experience. Writing romance is an exercise in opening yourself up—in feeling things very deeply and sharing those things in the form of a story. And this book made me FEEL. I hope it came across on the page, and I suppose the reality is, some people will feel it the way I did, and others won't. That's just how it goes. But for those who felt it—who laughed and cried along with Brax and Ky—know that I felt it too. Every bit of this story, every emotion, was real and raw and beautiful for me.

So where did it come from?

I had this idea about a trio—a brother and sister, and their best friend. What if (my ideas usually start with what if questions) the brother was in love with the best friend. And what if he'd loved her ever since he could remember, and he was kind of tortured by being just friends. And, what if he was devastatingly hot and had no trouble getting women, leading to his (well-deserved at this point) reputation as a player. But the only woman he really wanted was RIGHT THERE, and he couldn't have her. Oh yes, I like him already.

I wanted to write about a man who's kind of a bad boy—obviously not the dark, dangerous bad boy (there are lots of amazing authors who write that kind of hero far better than I could). But a bad boy who's a player. Hot, fun, confident—but he's not the guy you can date and think he's going to stick around. What made him interesting to me was *why*. Why would he be like that? I wanted it to be much deeper than "he can get away with it, so he does." Sure, he's gorgeous and likes to be naughty. But men can be gorgeous and naughty without leaving a long string of broken hearts in their wake.

But the things in his life that made him who he is when the story begins fit perfectly with the story I was envisioning. It's all about Kylie. He's never loved anyone else, and no one else will ever compare. But hell, he's a guy, and from a young age he had girls falling all over him. So he'd try one out—take her out, sleep with her, whatever. She wasn't Kylie. So he'd move on. After that kept happening, people in his life saw him a certain way. *Oh sure, that's just Braxton. He's such a player. He loves hot women, but nothing lasts.*

He lives that way for a long time, wearing the mask. Being the guy he thinks "his girls" need him to be. The man underneath was who really got to me as I was writing Braxton. He is fun and a little cocky. But he was also deeply wounded when his parents died, and he's spent his entire life hiding that part of himself. He shows his true self to Kylie in bits and pieces—tiny glimpses she's not sure how to interpret. There's a depth to him that she doesn't expect, and it disarms her every time. He wants to let her in so badly, and we see him try a little here and there.

Kylie's loved Braxton for as long as he's loved her, but she keeps that buried deep inside, not even acknowledging it to herself. It feels too dangerous to her, and who can blame her? She's seen him go through a lot of women, and she assumes that's just how he is.

In a lot of ways, Brax and Ky are already halfway to being a couple at the beginning of the book. They know all those little things about each other that couples would know. They have a comfort level with each other that is the result of years of friendship, and it skirts the very edge of something more. Ordering for each other at restaurants. Sharing food off each other's plates. Passing a cup of coffee back and forth without even thinking about it. I added moments like that very much on purpose. The characters don't think much of it, so as a reader, it might not have stuck out. Kylie doesn't protest when Braxton takes her coffee out of her hand and drinks it, for example. He hands it back and she drinks some, because it's something they would do all the time. Tiny moments like that were designed to show that they're so comfortable with each other, they do things that usually only romantic couples will do.

No wonder their dates never feel comfortable with their friendship...

Kylie wants something real. She feels like she's outgrowing her *let's party* life and wants to be with someone who has potential for a future. She has a good relationship with her father, and he taught her a lot about how she should be treated, simply by example. But she still has a hole left by her mother. She feels hurt and abandoned, and what she wants more than anything is the security of being loved. Despite what happened between her parents, she doesn't question the idea of love. She just doesn't see it right in front of her, in the form of her best friend.

This book, for me, was about highs and lows. Writing it was very much a roller coaster. The highs are pretty high. Braxton is desperately in love with her, and I was rooting for him to be with her from the beginning. Kylie's self-revelation that she's in love with him only made my desire to bring them together stronger. And when they do finally take that step—when Braxton's greatest wish becomes reality—OMG, the high. He's so happy. She's so happy. It's all so good and wonderful and did you maybe want to stop reading right about there?

The first time I had to take a break and breathe through my emotions as I wrote was when Brax lied to Selene about being with Kylie. I literally got up and paced around the room a few times, thinking, "Damn it Brax. Don't do it. This is going to be so baaaaad later." (And yes, I realize it's weird that I do things like that. I'm the one writing it, and it all only exists in my head at that point. Whatever. I'm okay with it.)

And when it came time to write the big crisis—the moment when Braxton breaks up with Kylie? Fucking hell, it was hard to write. I didn't want it to happen.

But that's what I mean about highs and lows. The highs made the lows harder, but ultimately it made the ending more satisfying.

I love this book, probably a little too much. It will always be special to me and I'm really glad I took the time to write it (it was literally the book I wasn't supposed to be writing for a while – it was not actually on my writing schedule, but like I said, sometimes the book demands it!). I hope you enjoyed it too!

CK

ALSO BY CLAIRE KINGSLEY

For a full and up-to-date listing of Claire Kingsley books visit www.clairekingsleybooks.com/books/

For comprehensive reading order, visit www.clairekingsleybooks.com/reading-order/

The Haven Brothers

Small-town romantic suspense with CK's signature endearing characters and heartwarming happily ever afters. Can be read as stand-alones.

Obsession Falls (Josiah and Audrey)

Storms and Secrets (Zachary and Marigold)

Temptation Trails (Garrett and Harper)

The rest of the Haven brothers will be getting their own happily ever afters!

How the Grump Saved Christmas (Elias and Isabelle)

A stand-alone, small-town Christmas romance.

The Bailey Brothers

Steamy, small-town family series with a dash of suspense. Five unruly brothers. Epic pranks. A quirky, feuding town. Big HEAs. Best read in order.

Protecting You (Asher and Grace part 1)

Fighting for Us (Asher and Grace part 2)

Unraveling Him (Evan and Fiona)

Rushing In (Gavin and Skylar)

Chasing Her Fire (Logan and Cara)

Rewriting the Stars (Levi and Annika)

The Miles Family

Sexy, sweet, funny, and heartfelt family series with a dash of suspense. Messy family. Epic bromance. Super romantic. Best read in order.

Broken Miles (Roland and Zoe)

Forbidden Miles (Brynn and Chase)

Reckless Miles (Cooper and Amelia)

Hidden Miles (Leo and Hannah)

Gaining Miles: A Miles Family Novella (Ben and Shannon)

Dirty Martini Running Club

Sexy, fun, feel-good romantic comedies with huge... hearts. Can be read as stand-alones.

Everly Dalton's Dating Disasters (Prequel with Everly, Hazel, and Nora)

Faking Ms. Right (Everly and Shepherd)

Falling for My Enemy (Hazel and Corban)

Marrying Mr. Wrong (Sophie and Cox)

Flirting with Forever (Nora and Dex)

Bluewater Billionaires

Hot romantic comedies. Lady billionaire BFFs and the badass heroes who love them. Can be read as stand-alones.

The Mogul and the Muscle (Cameron and Jude)

The Price of Scandal, Wild Open Hearts, and Crazy for Loving You

More Bluewater Billionaire shared-world romantic comedies by Lucy Score, Kathryn Nolan, and Pippa Grant

Bootleg Springs

by Claire Kingsley and Lucy Score

Hot and hilarious small-town romcom series with a dash of mystery and suspense. Best read in order.

Whiskey Chaser (Scarlett and Devlin)

Sidecar Crush (Jameson and Leah Mae)

Moonshine Kiss (Bowie and Cassidy)

Bourbon Bliss (June and George)

Gin Fling (Jonah and Shelby)

Highball Rush (Gibson and I can't tell you)

Book Boyfriends

Hot romcoms that will make you laugh and make you swoon. Can be read as stand-alones.

Book Boyfriend (Alex and Mia)

Cocky Roommate (Weston and Kendra)

Hot Single Dad (Caleb and Linnea)

Finding Ivy (William and Ivy)

A unique contemporary romance with a hint of mystery. Stand-alone.

His Heart (Sebastian and Brooke)

A poignant and emotionally intense story about grief, loss, and the transcendent power of love. Stand-alone.

The Always Series

Smoking hot, dirty talking bad boys with some angsty intensity. Can be read as stand-alones.

Always Have (Braxton and Kylie)

Always Will (Selene and Ronan)

Always Ever After (Braxton and Kylie)

The Jetty Beach Series

Sexy small-town romance series with swoony heroes, romantic HEAs, and lots of big feels. Can be read as stand-alones.

Behind His Eyes (Ryan and Nicole)

One Crazy Week (Melissa and Jackson)

Messy Perfect Love (Cody and Clover)

Operation Get Her Back (Hunter and Emma)

Weekend Fling (Finn and Juliet)

Good Girl Next Door (Lucas and Becca)

The Path to You (Gabriel and Sadie)

ABOUT THE AUTHOR

Claire Kingsley is a #1 Amazon bestselling author of sexy, heartwarming contemporary romance, romantic comedies, and small-town romantic suspense. She writes sassy, quirky heroines, swoony heroes who love big, romantic happily ever afters, and all the big feels.

She can't imagine life without coffee, great books, and the characters who inhabit her imagination. She lives in the inland Pacific Northwest with her three kids.

www.clairekingsleybooks.com

Printed in Dunstable, United Kingdom

76710343R00153